MY GOTHIC HEART

MY
GOTHIC
HEART

Selection, introduction and
arrangement by
CHARLIE
CASTELLETTI

MACMILLAN COLLECTOR'S LIBRARY

This collection first published 2023 by Macmillan Collector's Library
an imprint of Pan Macmillan
The Smithson, 6 Briset Street, London ECIM 5NR
EU representative: Macmillan Publishers Ireland Ltd,
1st Floor, The Liffey Trust Centre, 117–126 Sheriff Street Upper,
Dublin 1, DOI YC43
Associated companies throughout the world
www.panmacmillan.com

ISBN 978-1-0350-0261-0

Selection and arrangement
copyright © Macmillan Publishers International Ltd. 2023

Introduction and 'Epilogue' copyright © Charlie Castelletti 2023

The Permissions Acknowledgements on p. 213 constitute an
extension of this copyright page.

1 3 5 7 9 8 6 4 2

A CIP catalogue record for this book is available from the British Library.

Cover and endpaper design: Lucy Scholes, Pan Macmillan Art Department
Typeset in Plantin by Jouve (UK), Milton Keynes
Printed and bound in China by Imago

Visit www.panmacmillan.com to read more
about all our books and to buy them.

Contents

YET EACH MAN KILLS THE THING HE LOVES, BY EACH LET THIS BE HEARD

THERE IS NOTHING THAT ART CANNOT EXPRESS

THE LINE OF BEAUTY

A DREAM OF DEATH

FAR SAFER, OF A MIDNIGHT,
MEETING EXTERNAL GHOST

THE EARTH IS A TOMB, THE GAUDY SKY A VAULT, WE BUT WALKING CORPSES

MORE BEAUTIFUL THAN MOON OR STAR

Introduction
CHARLIE CASTELLETTI

When one hears the term 'Gothic', a few associations come to mind: uninhabitable terrain and moorland; castles, abandoned fortresses and abbeys; anything supernatural, the uncanny; problematic anti-heroes; heightened emotion and manipulation; melodramatic narrative arcs; dread, fear and a whole lot more. At the same time, while reliant on this generic register, there is no singular element that marks a text as Gothic. What the Gothic does is take everything we know about this world (and everything we don't) to its absolute breaking point. Its extremity transcends the limits of our bodies, intensifies our deeply held emotions, and examines the possibility of an afterlife, and what or who is to be found there.

The Gothic, as we know it today, has come to encompass a mood, an aesthetic. Through my selections, I have taken liberty with the term Gothic and, at specific moments, expanded outward of any typical convention or time period. Instead, I have been led by instinct, by the heart, allowing the Gothic to encompass what some might call a *vibe*. To punctuate the literary macabre with a few light-hearted selections allows for side-by-side pairings to illuminate something new in each of the passages. What do we see in Wilfred Owen's letter to Siegfried Sassoon when read alongside Catherine's highly charged declaration of identity in her attachment to Heathcliff? What might the Governess of Henry James's novella *The Turn of the Screw* have to say about Catherine Moreland's naivety when roaming around Northanger Abbey?

While you can expect to find extracts from well-known Gothic writers, such as Ann Radcliffe, Bram Stoker, the Brontë sisters, Joseph Sheridan Le Fanu, Percy Shelley and John Keats, you will also find snippets from writers less likely to be included alongside them, such as Christopher Marlowe, Virginia Woolf, Jane Austen and George Eliot.

My Gothic Heart is arranged into eight sections, each denoting an aspect of what we might consider to be Gothic in feeling. The first section, 'Into the dark I go and heed not where, so that I come again at last to thee', explores the ways in which we are seeking to unite in, or return to, something akin to love. The second, 'What's this flesh?', explores not only the limits on our bodies, but also the struggles we might endure within them. As Virginia Woolf put it in her novel *The Waves*, sometimes we 'have to bang [our] head against some hard door to call [ourselves] back to the body.' The third section, 'Yet each man kills the thing he loves, by each let this be heard', explores the extreme and often violent ways in which emotions are manifested through literature, an approach which, though not without its problems, is rooted in a desire to capture and conquer something, or someone. The extracts in the fourth, 'There is nothing that art cannot express', from Oscar Wilde's novel *The Picture of Dorian Gray*, demonstrate to us art's many capabilities. Fifth, 'The Line of Beauty'; a short, aesthetic endeavour. Sixth, 'A Dream of Death' explores the Gothic's obsession with life, death and everything that might come after. The seventh section, 'Far safer, of a midnight meeting, external ghost', from Emily Dickinson's poem, posits that there are far scarier things than the ghosts we have been taught to fear. The eighth, 'The earth is a tomb, the gaud sky a vault, we but walking corpses', builds on the previous section to explore the clash between the worldly and the supernatural, that sometimes, these two planes intersect. Lastly, 'More beautiful than moon or star' shows us that there is beauty to be found even in the darkness of the world.

Inspired as I am by the literature herein, and having researched a large proportion of the poems and texts from my sickbed (a most fitting setting to be cosied up in bed with hot chocolate and Netflix), I have chosen to end this anthology with a poem written in the throes of compiling this book.

What do I take from this literature as a person living in the twenty-first century? All of these texts are certainly of their time: the dangerous tropes, the problematic assertions and lack of authentic representation; they are there to be interrogated and for us to take issue with.

However, we still read them to this day, we understand these disturbing tales and our emotions continue to be stirred. The sentiment of Gothic literature and the heightened feelings explored within these literary works lives on, because love and death, worry and fear, misery and heartache: these are things that touch us and affect us all. These literary ghosts of the past haunt us. What do we want to say back?

INTO THE DARK I GO AND
HEED NOT WHERE SO THAT
I COME AGAIN AT LAST
TO THEE

from Carmilla

"You are afraid to die?"

"Yes, everyone is."

"But to die as lovers may – to die together, so
that they may live together."

Joseph Sheridan Le Fanu

Without Her

What of her glass without her? The blank gray
   There where the pool is blind of the
      moon's face.
   Her dress without her? The tossed empty
      space
Of cloud-rack whence the moon has passed
  away.
Her paths without her? Day's appointed sway
   Usurped by desolate night. Her pillowed
      place
   Without her? Tears, ah me! for love's good
      grace,
And cold forgetfulness of night or day.

What of the heart without her? Nay, poor heart,
   Of thee what word remains ere speech be still?
   A wayfarer by barren ways and chill,
Steep ways and weary, without her thou art,
Where the long cloud, the long wood's
  counterpart,
   Sheds doubled darkness up the labouring hill.

Dante Gabriel Rossetti

from Wuthering Heights

'If I were in heaven, Nelly, I should be extremely miserable.'

'Because you are not fit to go there,' I answered. 'All sinners would be miserable in heaven.'

'But it is not for that. I dreamt once that I was there.'

'I tell you I won't hearken to your dreams, Miss Catherine! I'll go to bed,' I interrupted again.

She laughed, and held me down; for I made a motion to leave my chair.

'This is nothing,' cried she: 'I was only going to say that heaven did not seem to be my home; and I broke my heart with weeping to come back to earth; and the angels were so angry that they flung me out into the middle of the heath on the top of Wuthering Heights; where I woke sobbing for joy. That will do to explain my secret, as well as the other. I've no more business to marry Edgar Linton than I have to be in heaven; and if the wicked man in there had not brought Heathcliff so low, I shouldn't have thought of it. It would degrade me to marry Heathcliff now; so he shall never know how I love him: and that, not because he's handsome, Nelly, but because he's more myself than I am. Whatever our souls are made of, his and mine are the same; and Linton's is as different as a moonbeam from lightning, or frost from fire.

[...]

I cannot express it; but surely you and everybody have a notion that there is or should be an existence of yours beyond you. What were the use of my creation, if I were entirely contained here? My great miseries in this world have been Heathcliff's miseries, and I watched and felt each from the beginning: my great thought in living is himself. If all else perished, and *he* remained, *I* should still continue to be; and if all else remained, and he were annihilated, the universe would turn to a mighty stranger: I should not seem a part of it. My love for Linton is like the foliage in the woods: time will change it, I'm well aware, as winter changes the trees. My love for Heathcliff resembles the eternal rocks beneath: a source of little visible delight, but necessary. Nelly, I *am* Heathcliff! He's always, always in my mind: not as a pleasure, any more than I am always a pleasure to myself, but as my own being. So don't talk of our separation again'.

Emily Brontë

My own Beloved, who hast lifted me

My own Beloved, who hast lifted me
From this drear flat of earth where I was thrown,
And in betwixt the languid ringlets, blown
A life-breath, till the forehead hopefully
Shines out again, as all the angels see,
Before thy saving kiss! My own, my own,
Who camest to me when the world was gone,
And I who looked for only God, found *thee!*
I find thee: I am safe, and strong, and glad.
As one who stands in dewless asphodel
Looks backward on the tedious time he had
In the upper life . . . so I, with bosom-swell,
Make witness here between the good and bad,
That Love, as strong as Death, retrieves as well.

Elizabeth Barrett Browning

from Edward II

EDWARD

  I cannot brook these haughty menaces:
  Am I a king and must be overruled?
  Brother, display my ensigns in the field;
  I'll bandy with the barons and the earls,
  And either die or live with Gaveston.

GAVESTON

  I can no longer keep me from my lord.
    [*He steps forward*]

EDWARD

  What, Gaveston! Welcome! Kiss not my hand;
  Embrace me, Gaveston, as I do thee!
  Why shouldst thou kneel; knowest thou not
    who I am?
  Thy friend, thy self, another Gaveston!
  Not Hylas was more mourned of Hercules
  Than thou hast been of me since thy exile.

GAVESTON

  And, since I went from hence, no soul in hell
  Hath felt more torment than poor Gaveston.

Christopher Marlowe

Letter from Wilfred Owen to Siegfried Sassoon

Know that since mid-September, when you still regarded me as a tiresome little knocker on your door, I held you as Keats + Christ + Elijah + my Colonel + my father-confessor + Amenophis IV in profile.

What's that mathematically?

In effect it is this: that I love you, dispassionately, so much, so *very* much, dear Fellow, that the blasting little smile you wear on reading this can't hurt me in the least.

If you consider what the above Names have severally done for me, you will know what you are doing. And you have *fixed* my Life—however short. You did not light me: I was always a mad comet; but you have fixed me. I spun round you a satellite for a month, but I shall swing out soon, a dark star in the orbit where you will blaze. It is some consolation to know that Jupiter himself sometimes swims out of Ken!

Wilfred Owen

from Adam Bede

"Adam," she said, "it is the Divine Will. My soul is so knit to yours that it is but a divided life I live without you. And this moment, now you are with me, and I feel that our hearts are filled with the same love, I have a fullness of strength to bear and do our heavenly Father's will, that I had lost before."

Adam paused and looked into her sincere, loving eyes.

"Then we'll never part any more, Dinah, till death parts us."

And they kissed each other with a deep joy.

What greater thing is there for two human souls, than to feel that they are joined for life—to strengthen each other in all labor, to rest on each other in all sorrow, to minister to each other in all pain, to be one with each other in silent unspeakable memories at the moment of the last parting?

George Eliot

The Travelling Companion

Into the silence of the empty night
I went, and took my scorned heart with me,
And all the thousand eyes of heaven were bright;
But Sorrow came and led me back to thee.

I turned my weary eyes towards the sun,
Out of the leaden East like smoke came he.
I laughed and said, "The night is past and
    done";
But Sorrow came and led me back to thee.

I turned my face towards the rising moon,
Out of the south she came most sweet to see,
She smiled upon my eyes that loathed the noon;
But Sorrow came and led me back to thee.

I bent my eyes upon the summer land,
And all the painted fields were ripe for me,
And every flower nodded to my hand;
But Sorrow came and led me back to thee.

O Love! O Sorrow! O desired Despair!
I turn my feet towards the boundless sea,
Into the dark I go and heed not where,
So that I come again at last to thee,

Lord Alfred Douglas

Roses and Rue
To L.L.

Could we dig up this long-buried treasure,
  Were it worth the pleasure,
We never could learn love's song,
  We are parted too long.

Could the passionate past that is fled
  Call back its dead,
Could we live it all over again,
  Were it worth the pain!

I remember we used to meet
  By an ivied seat,
And you warbled each pretty word
  With the air of a bird;

And your voice had a quaver in it,
  Just like a linnet,
And shook, as the blackbird's throat
  With its last big note;

And your eyes, they were green and grey
    Like an April day,
But lit into amethyst
    When I stooped and kissed;

And your mouth, it would never smile
    For a long, long while,
Then it rippled all over with laughter
    Five minutes after.

You were always afraid of a shower,
    Just like a flower:
I remember you started and ran
    When the rain began.

I remember I never could catch you,
    For no one could match you,
You had wonderful, luminous, fleet,
    Little wings to your feet.

I remember your hair – did I tie it?
    For it always ran riot –
Like a tangled sunbeam of gold:
    These things are old.

I remember so well the room,
  And the lilac bloom
That beat at the dripping pane
  In the warm June rain;

And the colour of your gown,
  It was amber-brown,
And two yellow satin bows
  From the shoulders rose.

And the handkerchief of French lace
  Which you held to your face –
Had a small tear left a stain?
  Or was it the rain?

On your hand as it waved adieu
  There were veins of blue;
In your voice as it said good-bye
  Was a petulant cry,

'You have only wasted your life'
  (Ah, that was the knife!)
When I rushed through the garden gate
  It was all too late.

Could we live it over again,
  Were it worth the pain,
Could the passionate past that is fled
  Call back its dead!

Well, if my heart must break,
  Dear love, for your sake,
It will break in music, I know,
  Poets' hearts break so.

But strange that I was not told
  That the brain can hold
In a tiny ivory cell,
  God's heaven and hell.

Oscar Wilde

from Jane Eyre

'Do you think I am an automaton? – a machine without feelings? and can bear to have my morsel of bread snatched from my lips, and my drop of living water dashed from my cup? Do you think, because I am poor, obscure, plain, and little, I am soulless and heartless? You think wrong! – I have as much soul as you – and full as much heart! And if God had gifted me with some beauty and much wealth, I should have made it as hard for you to leave me, as it is now for me to leave you. I am not talking to you now through the medium of custom, conventionalities, nor even of mortal flesh – it is my spirit that addresses your spirit; just as if both had passed through the grave, and we stood at God's feet, equal – as we are!'

Charlotte Brontë

'I cry your mercy, pity, love – ay, love!'

I cry your mercy, pity, love – ay, love!
Merciful love that tantalizes not,
One-thoughted, never-wandering, guileless love,
Unmasked, and being seen – without a blot!
O! let me have thee whole, – all, all, be mine!
That shape, that fairness, that sweet minor zest
Of love, your kiss – those hands, those eyes
   divine,
That warm, white, lucent, million-pleasured
   breast –
Yourself – your soul – in pity give me all,
Withhold no atom's atom or I die;
Or living on perhaps, your wretched thrall,
Forget, in the mist of idle misery,
Life's purposes – the palate of my mind
Losing its gust, and my ambition blind!

John Keats

WHAT'S THIS FLESH?

from The Duchess of Malfi

Bosola. I am come to make thy tomb.

Duchess. Hah, my tomb!
Thou speak'st as if I lay upon my death-bed,
Gasping for breath: dost thou perceive me sick?

Bosola. Yes, and the more dangerously, since thy
   sickness is insensible.

Duchess. Thou art not mad, sure—dost know me?

Bosola. Yes.

Duchess. Who am I?

Bosola. Thou art a box of worm-seed; at best,
   but a salvatory of green mummy. What's this
   flesh? A little crudded milk, fantastical puff-
   paste. Our bodies are weaker than those
   paper prisons boys use to keep flies in; more
   contemptible, since ours is to preserve earth-
   worms. Didst thou ever see a lark in a cage?
   Such is the soul in the body; this world is like
   her little turf of grass, and the heaven o'er
   our heads, like her looking-glass, only gives us
   a miserable knowledge of the small compass
   of our prison.

John Webster

Pain has an element of blank

Pain has an element of blank;
It cannot recollect
When it began, or if there were
A day when it was not.

It has no future but itself,
Its infinite realms contain
Its past, enlightened to perceive
New periods of pain.

Emily Dickinson

from The Mysteries of Udolpho

'O my Emily!' he resumed, after a long pause, 'I do then see you once again, and hear again the sound of that voice! I have haunted this place—these gardens, for many—many nights, with a faint, very faint hope of seeing you. This was the only chance that remained to me, and thank Heaven! it has at length succeeded—I am not condemned to absolute despair!'

Emily said something, she scarcely knew what, expressive of her unalterable affection, and endeavoured to calm the agitation of his mind; but Valancourt could for some time only utter incoherent expressions of his emotions; and, when he was somewhat more composed, he said, 'I came hither, soon after sunset, and have been watching in the gardens, and in this pavilion ever since; for, though I had now given up all hope of seeing you, I could not resolve to tear myself from a place so near to you, and should probably have lingered about the château till morning dawned. O how heavily the moments have passed, yet with what various emotion have they been marked, as I sometimes thought I heard footsteps, and fancied you were approaching, and then again—perceived only a dead and dreary silence! But, when you opened the door of the pavilion, and the darkness prevented my distinguishing with certainty, whether it was my love—my heart beat so strongly with hopes and fears, that I could not speak. The instant I heard the plaintive accents of your voice, my doubts vanished, but not my fears, till you spoke of me; then, losing the apprehension of alarming you in the excess of my emotion, I could no longer be silent. O Emily! these are moments, in which joy and grief struggle so powerfully for pre-eminence, that the heart can scarcely support the contest!'

Emily's heart acknowledged the truth of this assertion, but the joy she felt on thus meeting Valancourt, at the very moment when she was lamenting, that they must probably meet no more, soon melted into grief, as reflection stole over her thoughts, and imagination prompted visions of the future. She struggled to recover the calm dignity of mind, which was necessary to support her through this last interview, and which Valancourt found it utterly impossible to attain, for the transports of his joy changed abruptly into those of suffering, and he expressed in the most impassioned language his horror of this separation, and his despair of their ever meeting again. Emily wept silently as she listened to him, and then, trying to command her own distress, and to sooth his, she suggested every circumstance that could lead to hope. But the energy of his fears led him instantly to detect the friendly fallacies, which she endeavoured to impose on herself and him, and also to conjure up illusions too powerful for his reason.

'You are going from me,' said he, 'to a distant country, O how distant!—to new society, new friends, new admirers, with people too, who will try to make you forget me, and to promote new connections! How can I know this, and not know, that you will never return for me—never can be mine.' His voice was stifled by sighs.

'You believe, then,' said Emily, 'that the pangs I suffer proceed from a trivial and temporary interest; you believe—'

'Suffer!' interrupted Valancourt, 'suffer for me! O Emily—how sweet—how bitter are those words; what comfort, what anguish do they give!

I ought not to doubt the steadiness of your affection, yet such is the inconsistency of real love, that it is always awake to suspicion, however unreasonable; always requiring new assurances from the object of its interest, and thus it is, that I always feel revived, as by a new conviction, when your words tell me I am dear to you; and, wanting these, I relapse into doubt, and too often into despondency.' Then seeming to recollect himself, he exclaimed, 'But what a wretch am I, thus to torture you, and in these moments, too! I, who ought to support and comfort you!'

Ann Radcliffe

from Dr Jekyll and Mr Hydc

"My devil had been long caged, he came out
  roaring."

Robert Louis Stevenson

Parted Lips

Parted lips, between which love dwells –
    Only a little space of breath and shadow,
Yet here the gate of all the world to me

Edward Carpenter

To His Coy Mistress

Had we but world enough, and time,
This coyness, Lady, were no crime.
We would sit down, and think which way
To walk, and pass our long love's day.
Thou by the Indian Ganges' side
Shouldst rubies find; I by the tide
Of Humber would complain. I would
Love you ten years before the flood:
And you should, if you please, refuse
Till the conversion of the Jews.
My vegetable love should grow
Vaster than empires and more slow.
An hundred years should go to praise
Thine eyes, and on thy forehead gaze.
Two hundred to adore each breast:
But thirty thousand to the rest.
An age at least to every part,
And the last age should show your heart;
For, Lady, you deserve this state;
Nor would I love at lower rate.
  But at my back I always hear
Time's wingèd chariot hurrying near:
And yonder all before us lie

Deserts of vast eternity.
Thy beauty shall no more be found;
Nor, in thy marble vault, shall sound
My echoing song: then worms shall try
That long-preserved virginity,
And your quaint honour turn to dust;
And into ashes all my lust;
The grave's a fine and private place,
But none, I think, do there embrace.

  Now therefore, while the youthful hue
Sits on thy skin like morning dew,
And while thy willing soul transpires
At every pore with instant fires,
Now let us sport us while we may,
And now, like amorous birds of prey,
Rather at once our time devour
Than languish in his slow-chapped power.
Let us roll all our strength, and all
Our sweetness, up into one ball,
And tear our pleasures with rough strife,
Through the iron gates of life:
Thus, though we cannot make our sun
Stand still, yet we will make him run.

Andrew Marvell

from Lady Audley's Secret

Now love is so very subtle an essence, such an indefinable metaphysical marvel, that its due force, though very cruelly felt by the sufferer himself, is never clearly understood by those who look on at his torments and wonder why he takes the common fever so badly [...] He forgot that love, which is a madness, and a scourge, and a fever, and a delusion, and a snare, is also a mystery, and very imperfectly understood by every one except the individual sufferer who writhes under its tortures.

Mary Elizabeth Braddon

My Heart and I

I

ENOUGH! We're tired, my heart and I.
　We sit beside the headstone thus,
　And wish that name were carved for us.
The moss reprints more tenderly
　The hard types of the mason's knife,
　As heaven's sweet life renews earth's life
With which we're tired, my heart and I.

II

You see we're tired, my heart and I.
　We dealt with books, we trusted men,
　And in our own blood drenched the pen,
As if such colours could not fly.
　We walked too straight for fortune's end,
　We loved too true to keep a friend;
At last we're tired, my heart and I.

III

How tired we feel, my heart and I!
　We seem of no use in the world;
　Our fancies hang grey and uncurled

About men's eyes indifferently;
    Our voice which thrilled you so, will let
    You sleep; our tears are only wet:
What do we here, my heart and I?

IV

So tired, so tired, my heart and I!
    It was not thus in that old time
    When Ralph sat with me 'neath the lime
To watch the sunset from the sky.
    "Dear love, you're looking tired," he said;
    I, smiling at him, shook my head:
'Tis now we're tired, my heart and I.

V

So tired, so tired, my heart and I!
    Though now none takes me on his arm
    To fold me close and kiss me warm
Till each quick breath end in a sigh
    Of happy languor. Now, alone,
    We lean upon this graveyard stone,
Uncheered, unkissed, my heart and I.

VI

Tired out we are, my heart and I.
  Suppose the world brought diadems
  To tempt us, crusted with loose gems
Of powers and pleasures? Let it try.
  We scarcely care to look at even
  A pretty child, or God's blue heaven,
We feel so tired, my heart and I.

VII

Yet who complains? My heart and I?
  In this abundant earth no doubt
  Is little room for things worn out:
Disdain them, break them, throw them by
  And if before the days grew rough
  We *once* were loved, used,—well enough,
I think, we've fared, my heart and I.

Elizabeth Barrett Browning

from A Tale of Two Cities

'I would ask you to believe that he has a heart he very, very seldom reveals, and that there are deep wounds in it. My dear, I have seen it bleeding.'

Charles Dickens

from The Tenant of Wildfell Hall

'There is such a thing as looking through a person's eyes into the heart, and learning more of the height, and breadth, and depth of another's soul in one hour than, it might take you a lifetime to discover, if he or she were not disposed to reveal it, or if you had not the sense to understand it.'

Anne Brontë

What would I give?

What would I give for a heart of flesh to warm
  me through,
Instead of this heart of stone ice-cold whatever
  I do;
Hard and cold and small, of all hearts the worst
  of all.

What would I give for words, if only words
  would come;
But now in its misery my spirit has fallen dumb:
O, merry friends, go your way, I have never a
  word to say.

What would I give for tears, not smiles but
  scalding tears,
To wash the black mark clean, and to thaw the
  frost of years,
To wash the stain ingrain and to make me clean
  again.

Christina Rossetti

Oh, they have robbed me of the hope

Oh, they have robbed me of the hope
My spirit held so dear;
They will not let me hear that voice
My soul delights to hear.
They will not let me see that face
I so delight to see;
And they have taken all thy smiles,
And all thy love from me.

Well, let them seize on all they can:—
One treasure still is mine,—
A heart that loves to think on thee,
And feels the worth of thine.

Anne Brontë

Time to Come

O, Death! a black and pierceless pall
　　Hangs round thee, and the future state;
No eye may see, no mind may grasp
　　That mystery of fate.

This brain, which now alternate throbs
　　With swelling hope and gloomy fear;
This heart, with all the changing hues,
　　That mortal passions bear—

This curious frame of human mould,
　　Where unrequited cravings play,
This brain, and heart, and wondrous form
　　Must all alike decay.

The leaping blood will stop its flow;
　　The hoarse death-struggle pass; the cheek
Lay bloomless, and the liquid tongue
　　Will then forget to speak.

The grave will take me; earth will close
  O'er cold dull limbs and ashy face;
But where, O, Nature, where shall be
  The soul's abiding place?

Will it e'en live? For though its light
  Must shine till from the body torn;
Then, when the oil of life is spent,
  Still shall the taper burn?

O, powerless is this struggling brain
  To rend the mighty mystery;
In dark, uncertain awe it waits
  The common doom, to die.

Walt Whitman

I wake and feel the fell of dark, not day

I wake and feel the fell of dark, not day.
What hours, O what black hours we have spent
This night! what sights you, heart, saw; ways
   you went!
And more must, in yet longer light's delay.

With witness I speak this. But where I say
Hours I mean years, mean life. And my lament
Is cries countless, cries like dead letters sent
To dearest him that lives alas! away.

I am gall, I am heartburn. God's most deep
   decree
Bitter would have me taste: my taste was me;
Bones built in me, flesh filled, blood brimmed
   the curse.
Selfyeast of spirit a dull dough sours. I see
The lost are like this, and their scourge to be
As I am mine, their sweating selves; but worse.

Gerard Manley Hopkins

from Jane Eyre

'I sometimes have a queer feeling with regard to you – especially when you are near me, as now: it is as if I had a string somewhere under my left ribs, tightly and inextricably knotted to a similar string situated in the corresponding quarter of your little frame. And if that boisterous Channel, and two hundred miles or so of land come broad between us, I am afraid that cord of communion will be snapped; and then I've a nervous notion I should take to bleeding inwardly. As for you – you'd forget me.'

Charlotte Brontë

A Man Who Died

Ah stern, cold man,
How can you lie so relentless hard
While I wash you with weeping water!
Do you set your face against the daughter
Of life? Can you never discard
Your curt pride's ban?

You masquerader!
How can you shame to act this part
Of unswerving indifference to me?
You want at last, ah me!
To break my heart,
Evader!

You know your mouth
Was always sooner to soften
Even than your eyes.
Now shut it lies
Relentless, however often
I kiss it in drouth.

It has no breath
Nor any relaxing. Where,
Where are you, what have you done?
What is this mouth of stone?
How did you dare
Take cover in death!

Once you could see,
The white moon show like a breast revealed
By the slipping shawl of stars.
Could see the small stars tremble
As the heart beneath did wield
Systole, diastole.

All the lovely macrocosm
Was woman once to you,
Bride to your groom.
No tree in bloom
But it leaned you a new
White bosom.

And always and ever
Soft as a summering tree
Unfolds from the sky, for your good,
Unfolded womanhood:
Shedding you down as a tree
Sheds its flowers on a river.

I saw your brows
Set like rocks beside a sea of gloom,
And I shed my very soul down into your
    thought:
Like flowers I fell to be caught
On the comforted pool, like bloom
That leaves the boughs.

Oh, masquerader!
With a hard face white-enamelled,
What are you now?
Do you care no longer how
My heart is trammelled,
Evader?

Is this you, after all,
Metallic, obdurate,
With bowels of steel?
Did you *never* feel?—
Cold, insensate,
Mechanical?

Ah, no!—you multiform,
You that I loved, you wonderful,
You who darkened and shone,
You were many men in one;
But never this null
This never-warm!

Is this the sum of you?
Is it all naught?
Cold, metal-cold?
Are you all told
Here, iron-wrought?
Is this what's become of you?

D. H. Lawrence

*YET EACH MAN KILLS THE
THING HE LOVES, BY EACH
LET THIS BE HEARD*

Porphyria's Lover

The rain set early in to-night,
  The sullen wind was soon awake,
It tore the elm-tops down for spite,
  And did its worst to vex the lake:
  I listened with heart fit to break.
When glided in Porphyria; straight
  She shut the cold out and the storm,
And kneeled and made the cheerless grate
  Blaze up, and all the cottage warm;
  Which done, she rose, and from her form
Withdrew the dripping cloak and shawl,
  And laid her soiled gloves by, untied
Her hat and let the damp hair fall,
  And, last, she sat down by my side
  And called me. When no voice replied,
She put my arm about her waist,
  And made her smooth white shoulder bare,
And all her yellow hair displaced,
  And, stooping, made my cheek lie there,
  And spread, o'er all, her yellow hair,
Murmuring how she loved me—she
  Too weak, for all her heart's endeavour,

To set its struggling passion free
    From pride, and vainer ties dissever,
    And give herself to me for ever.
But passion sometimes would prevail,
    Nor could to-night's gay feast restrain
A sudden thought of one so pale
    For love of her, and all in vain:
    So, she was come through wind and rain.
Be sure I looked up at her eyes
    Happy and proud; at last I knew
Porphyria worshipped me; surprise
    Made my heart swell, and still it grew
    While I debated what to do.
That moment she was mine, mine, fair,
    Perfectly pure and good: I found
A thing to do, and all her hair
    In one long yellow string I wound
    Three times her little throat around,
And strangled her. No pain felt she;
    I am quite sure she felt no pain.
As a shut bud that holds a bee,
    I warily oped her lids: again
    Laughed the blue eyes without a stain.
And I untightened next the tress
    About her neck; her cheek once more

Blushed bright beneath my burning kiss:
  I propped her head up as before,
  Only, this time my shoulder bore
Her head, which droops upon it still:
  The smiling rosy little head,
So glad it has its utmost will,
  That all it scorned at once is fled,
  And I, its love, am gained instead!
Porphyria's love: she guessed not how
  Her darling one wish would be heard.
And thus we sit together now,
  And all night long we have not stirred,
  And yet God has not said a word!

Robert Browning

from Wuthering Heights

'You teach me now how cruel you've been – cruel and false. *Why* did you despise me? *Why* did you betray your own heart, Cathy? I have not one word of comfort. You deserve this. You have killed yourself. Yes, you may kiss me, and cry; and wring out my kisses and tears: they'll blight you – they'll damn you. You loved me – then what *right* had you to leave me? What right – answer me – for the poor fancy you felt for Linton? Because misery, and degradation, and death, and nothing that God or Satan could inflict would have parted us, *you*, of your own will, did it. I have not broken your heart – *you* have broken it; and in breaking it, you have broken mine. So much the worse for me, that I am strong. Do I want to live? What kind of living will it be when you – oh, God! Would *you* like to live with your soul in the grave?'

'Let me alone. Let me alone,' sobbed Catherine. 'If I've done wrong, I'm dying for it. It is enough! You left me too: but I won't upbraid you! I forgive you. Forgive me!'

'It is hard to forgive, and to look at those eyes

and feel those wasted hands,' he answered. 'Kiss me again; and don't let me see your eyes! I forgive what you have done to me. I love *my* murderer – but *yours*! How can I?'

Charlotte Brontë

from Romeo and Juliet

For here lies Juliet, and her beauty makes
This vault a feasting presence full of light.
Death, lie thou there, by a dead man interr'd.

      [*Laying* PARIS *in the tomb.*

How oft when men are at the point of death
Have they been merry! which their keepers call
A lightning before death: O, how may I
Call this a lightning! O my love! my wife!
Death, that hath suck'd the honey of thy breath,
Hath had no power yet upon thy beauty:
Thou art not conquer'd; beauty's ensign yet
Is crimson in thy lips and in thy cheeks,
And death's pale flag is not advanced there.
Tybalt, liest thou there in thy bloody sheet?
O, what more favour can I do to thee,
Than with that hand that cut thy youth in twain
To sunder his that was thy enemy?
Forgive me, cousin!—Ah, dear Juliet,
Why art thou yet so fair? shall I believe
That unsubstantial Death is amorous;
And that the lean abhorred monster keeps
Thee here in dark to be his paramour?
For fear of that, I still will stay with thee;

And never from this palace of dim night
Depart again: here, here will I remain
With worms that are thy chamber-maids; O,
   here
Will I set up my everlasting rest;
And shake the yoke of inauspicious stars
From this world-wearied flesh.—Eyes, look your
   last!
Arms, take your last embrace! and, lips, O you
The doors of breath, seal with a righteous kiss
A dateless bargain to engrossing death!—
Come, bitter conduct, come, unsavoury guide!
Thou desperate pilot, now at once run on
The dashing rocks thy sea-sick weary bark!
Here's to my love. [*drinks*]—O true apothecary!
Thy drugs are quick.—Thus with a kiss I die.

                               [*Dies.*

William Shakespeare

from The Ballad of Reading Gaol

I

He did not wear his scarlet coat,
　For blood and wine are red,
And blood and wine were on his hands
　When they found him with the dead,
The poor dead woman whom he loved,
　And murdered in her bed.

He walked amongst the Trial Men
　In a suit of shabby grey;
A cricket cap was on his head,
　And his step seemed light and gay;
But I never saw a man who looked
　So wistfully at the day.

I never saw a man who looked
　With such a wistful eye
Upon that little tent of blue
　Which prisoners call the sky,
And at every drifting cloud that went
　With sails of silver by.

I walked, with other souls in pain,
 Within another ring,
And was wondering if the man had done
 A great or little thing,
When a voice behind me whispered low,
 'That fellow's got to swing.'

Dear Christ! the very prison walls
 Suddenly seemed to reel,
And the sky above my head became
 Like a casque of scorching steel;
And, though I was a soul in pain,
 My pain I could not feel.

I only knew what hunted thought
 Quickened his step, and why
He looked upon the garish day
 With such a wistful eye;
The man had killed the thing he loved
 And so he had to die.

Yet each man kills the thing he loves,
 By each let this be heard,
Some do it with a bitter look,
 Some with a flattering word,

The coward does it with a kiss,
    The brave man with a sword!

Some kill their love when they are young,
    And some when they are old;
Some strangle with the hands of Lust,
    Some with the hands of Gold:
The kindest use a knife, because
    The dead so soon grow cold.

Some love too little, some too long,
    Some sell, and others buy;
Some do the deed with many tears,
    And some without a sigh:
For each man kills the thing he loves,
    Yet each man does not die.

He does not die a death of shame
    On a day of dark disgrace,
Nor have a noose about his neck,
    Nor a cloth upon his face,
Nor drop feet foremost through the floor
    Into an empty space.

He does not sit with silent men
  Who watch him night and day;
Who watch him when he tries to weep,
  And when he tries to pray;
Who watch him lest himself should rob
  The prison of its prey.

He does not wake at dawn to see
  Dread figures throng his room,
The shivering Chaplain robed in white,
  The Sheriff stern with gloom,
And the Governor all in shiny black,
  With the yellow face of Doom.

He does not rise in piteous haste
  To put on convict-clothes,
While some coarse-mouthed Doctor gloats, and
    notes
  Each new and nerve-twitched pose,
Fingering a watch whose little ticks
  Are like horrible hammer-blows.

He does not know that sickening thirst
  That sands one's throat, before
The hangman with his gardener's gloves
  Comes through the padded door,
And binds one with three leathern thongs,
  That the throat may thirst no more.

He does not bend his head to hear
  The Burial Office read,
Nor, while the terror of his soul
  Tells him he is not dead,
Cross his own coffin, as he moves
  Into the hideous shed.

He does not stare upon the air
  Through a little roof of glass:
He does not pray with lips of clay
  For his agony to pass;
Nor feel upon his shuddering cheek
  The kiss of Caiaphas.

Oscar Wilde

Love and Death

I watch'd thee when the foe was at our side,
Ready to strike at him—or thee and me,
Were safety hopeless—rather than divide
Aught with one loved save love and liberty.

I watch'd thee on the breakers, when the rock
Received our prow, and all was storm and fear,
And bade thee cling to me through every shock;
This arm would be thy bark, or breast thy bier.

I watch'd thee when the fever glazed thine eyes,
Yielding my couch and stretch'd me on the
    ground,
When overworn with watching, ne'er to rise
From thence if thou an early grave hadst found.

The earthquake came, and rock'd the quivering
    wall,
And men and nature reel'd as if with wine.
Whom did I seek around the tottering hall?
For thee. Whose safety first provide for?
    Thine.

And when convulsive throes denied my breath
The faintest utterance to my fading thought,
To thee—to thee—e'en in the gasp of death
My spirit turn'd, oh! oftener than it ought.

Thus much and more; and yet thou lov'st
    me not,
And never wilt! Love dwells not in our will.
Nor can I blame thee, though it be my lot
To strongly, wrongly, vainly love thee still.

George, Lord Byron

He wishes his Beloved were Dead

Were you but lying cold and dead,
And lights were paling out of the West,
You would come hither, and bend your head,
And I would lay my head on your breast;
And you would murmur tender words,
Forgiving me, because you were dead:
Nor would you rise and hasten away,
Though you have the will of the wild birds,
But know your hair was bound and wound
About the stars and moon and sun:
O would, beloved, that you lay
Under the dock-leaves in the ground,
While lights were paling one by one.

W. B. Yeats

from Carmilla

She used to place her pretty arms about my neck, draw me to her, and laying her cheek to mine, murmur with her lips near my ear, "Dearest, your little heart is wounded; think me not cruel because I obey the irresistible law of my strength and weakness; if your dear heart is wounded, my wild heart bleeds with yours. In the rapture of my enormous humiliation I live in your warm life, and you shall die—die, sweetly die—into mine. I cannot help it; as I draw near to you, you, in your turn, will draw near to others, and learn the rapture of that cruelty, which yet is love; so, for a while, seek to know no more of me and mine, but trust me with all your loving spirit."

And when she had spoken such a rhapsody, she would press me more closely in her trembling embrace, and her lips in soft kisses gently glow upon my cheek.

Her agitations and her language were unintelligible to me.

From these foolish embraces, which were not of very frequent occurrence, I must allow, I used to wish to extricate myself; but my energies seemed to fail me. Her murmured words sounded like a lullaby in my ear, and soothed my resistance into a trance, from which I only seemed to recover myself when she withdrew her arms.

In these mysterious moods I did not like her. I experienced a strange tumultuous excitement that was pleasurable, ever and anon, mingled with a vague sense of fear and disgust. I had no distinct thoughts about her while such scenes lasted, but I was conscious of a love growing into adoration, and also of abhorrence. This I know is paradox, but I can make no other attempt to explain the feeling.

[...]

Sometimes after an hour of apathy, my strange and beautiful companion would take my hand and hold it with a fond pressure, renewed again and again; blushing softly, gazing in my face with languid and burning eyes, and breathing so fast that her dress rose and fell with the tumultuous respiration. It was like the ardor of a lover; it embarrassed me; it was hateful and yet overpowering; and with gloating eyes she drew me to her, and her hot lips traveled along my cheek in kisses; and she would whisper, almost in sobs, "You are mine, you *shall* be mine, and you and I are one forever." Then she would throw herself back in her chair, with her small hands over her eyes, leaving me trembling.

Sheridan Le Fanu

from The Monk

The monks retired immediately, and Matilda and the abbot remained together.

'What have you done, imprudent woman!' exclaimed the latter, as soon as they were left alone. 'Tell me, are my suspicions just? Am I indeed to lose you? Has your own hand been the instrument of your destruction?'

She smiled, and grasped his hand. 'In what have I been imprudent, Father? I have sacrificed a pebble, and saved a diamond: my death preserves a life valuable to the world and more dear to me than my own. Yes, Father, I am poisoned; but know that the poison once circulated in your veins.'

'Matilda!'

'What I tell you I resolved never to discover to you but on the bed of death: that moment is now arrived. You cannot have forgotten the day already, when your life was endangered by the bite of a *cientipedoro*. The physician gave you over, declaring himself ignorant how to extract the venom: I knew but of one means, and hesitated not a moment to employ it. I was left alone with you: you slept; I loosened the bandage from your hand; I kissed the wound, and drew out the poison with my lips. The effect has been more sudden than I expected. I feel death at my heart; yet an hour, and I shall be in a better world.'

'Almighty God!' exclaimed the abbot, and sank almost lifeless upon the bed.

After a few minutes he again raised himself up suddenly, and gazed upon Matilda with all the wildness of despair.

'And you have sacrificed yourself for me! You die, and die to preserve Ambrosio! And is there indeed no remedy, Matilda? And is there indeed no hope? Speak to me, oh! speak to me! Tell me that you have still the means of life!'

'Be comforted, my only friend! Yes, I have still the means of life in my power: but 'tis a means which I dare not employ. It is dangerous! It is dreadful! Life would be purchased at too dear a rate . . . unless it were permitted me to live for you.'

'Then live for me, Matilda, for me and gratitude!' – (he caught her hand, and pressed it rapturously to his lips.) – 'Remember our late conversations; I now consent to everything:

remember in what lively colours you described the union of souls; be it ours to realise those ideas. Let us forget the distinctions of sex, despise the world's prejudices, and only consider each other as brother and friend. Live then, Matilda! Oh! live for me!'

'Ambrosio, it must not be. When I thought thus, I deceived both you and myself. Either I must die at present, or expire by the lingering torments of unsatisfied desire. Oh! since we last conversed together, a dreadful veil has been rent from before my eyes. I love you no longer with the devotion which is paid to a saint: I prize you no more for the virtues of your soul; I lust for the enjoyment of your person. The woman reigns in my bosom, and I am become prey to the wildest of passions. Away with friendship! 'tis a cold unfeeling word. My bosom burns with love, with unutterable love, and love must be its return. Tremble then, Ambrosio, tremble to succeed in your prayers. If I live, your truth, your reputation, your reward of a life passed in sufferings, all that you value is irretrievably lost. I shall no longer be able to combat my passions, shall seize every opportunity to excite your desires, and labour to effect your dishonour and my own. No. no, Ambrosio; I must not live! I am convinced with every moment, that I have but one alternative; I feel with every heart-throb, that I must enjoy you, or die.'

'Amazement! – Matilda! can it be you who speak to me?'

He made a movement as if to quit his seat. She uttered a loud shriek, and raising herself half out of the bed, threw her arms round the friar to detain him.

'Oh! do not leave me! Listen to my errors with compassion! In a few hours I shall be no more; yet a little, and I am free from this disgraceful passion.'

'Wretched woman, what can I say to you? I cannot . . . I must not . . . But live, Matilda! Oh! live!'

Matthew Lewis

from Dracula

To one thing I have made up my mind: if we find out that Mina must be a vampire in the end, then she shall not go into that unknown and terrible land alone. I suppose it is thus that in old times one vampire meant many; just as their hideous bodies could only rest in sacred earth, so the holiest love was the recruiting sergeant for their ghastly ranks.

Bram Stoker

The Apparition

When by thy scorn, O murd'ress, I am dead
    And that thou think'st thee free
From all solicitation from me
Then shall my ghost come to thy bed,
And thee, feign'd vestal, in worse arms shall see;
Then thy sick taper will begin to wink,
And he, whose thou art then, being tir'd before,
Will, if thou stir, or pinch to wake him, think
    Thou call'st for more,
And in false sleep will from thee shrink;
And then, poor aspen wretch, neglected thou
Bath'd in a cold quicksilver sweat wilt lie
    A verier ghost than I.
What I will say, I will not tell thee now,
Lest that preserve thee; and since my love is
   spent,
I'had rather thou shouldst painfully repent,
Than by my threat'nings rest still innocent.

John Donne

from Frankenstein

'You must create a female for me, with whom I can live in the interchange of those sympathies necessary for my being. This you alone can do; and I demand it of you as a right which you must not refuse to concede.'

The latter part of his tale had kindled anew in me the anger that had died away while he narrated his peaceful life among the cottagers, and, as he said this, I could no longer suppress the rage that burned within me.

'I do refuse it,' I replied; 'and no torture shall ever extort a consent from me. You may render me the most miserable of men, but you shall never make me base in my own eyes. Shall I create another like yourself, whose joint wickedness might desolate the world! Begone! I have answered you; you may torture me, but I will never consent.'

'You are in the wrong,' replied the fiend; 'and, instead of threatening, I am content to reason with you. I am malicious because I am miserable. Am I not shunned and hated by all mankind? You, my creator, would tear me to pieces, and triumph; remember that, and tell me why I should pity man more than he pities me? You would not call it murder if you could precipitate me into one of those ice-rifts, and destroy my frame, the work of your own hands. Shall I respect man when he condemns me? Let him live with me in the interchange of kindness; and, instead of injury, I would bestow every benefit upon him with tears of gratitude at his acceptance. But that cannot be; the human senses are insurmountable barriers to our union. Yet mine shall not be the submission of abject slavery. I will revenge my injuries: if I cannot inspire love, I will cause fear; and chiefly towards you, my arch-enemy, because my creator, do I swear inextinguishable hatred. Have a care: I will work at your destruction, nor finish until I desolate your heart, so that you shall curse the hour of your birth.'

A fiendish rage animated him as he said this; his face was wrinkled into contortions too horrible for human eyes to behold; but presently he calmed himself and proceeded, 'I intended to reason. This passion is detrimental to me; for you do not reflect that *you* are the cause of its excess.

If any being felt emotions of benevolence towards me, I should return them a hundred and a hundredfold; for that one creature's sake, I would make peace with the whole kind! But I now indulge in dreams of bliss that cannot be realised. What I ask of you is reasonable and moderate; I demand a creature of another sex, but as hideous as myself; the gratification is small, but it is all that I can receive, and it shall content me. It is true we shall be monsters, cut off from all the world; but on that account we shall be more attached to one another. Our lives will not be happy, but they will be harmless, and free from the misery I now feel. Oh! my creator, make me happy; let me feel gratitude towards you for one benefit! Let me see that I excite the sympathy of some existing thing; do not deny me my request!'

Mary Shelley

The Kind Ghosts

She sleeps on soft, last breaths; but no ghost
  looms
Out of the stillness of her palace wall,
Her wall of boys on boys and dooms on dooms.

She dreams of golden gardens and sweet
  glooms,
Not marvelling why her roses never fall
Nor what red mouths were torn to make their
  blooms.

The shades keep down which well might roam
  her hall.
Quiet their blood lies in her crimson rooms
And she is not afraid of their footfall.

They move not from her tapestries, their pall,
Nor pace her terraces, their hecatombs,
Lest aught she be disturbed, or grieved at all.

Wilfred Owen

THERE IS NOTHING THAT ART
CANNOT EXPRESS

Words on the window-pane

Did she in summer write it, or in spring,
    Or with this wail of autumn at her ears,
    Or in some winter left among old years
Scratched it through tettered cark? A certain
    thing
That round her heart the frost was hardening,
    Not to be thawed of tears, which on this
      pane
    Channelled the rime, perchance, in fevered
      rain,
For false man's sake and love's most bitter sting.

Howbeit, between this last word and the next
Unwritten, subtly seasoned was the smart,
    And here at least the grace to weep: if she,
Rather, midway in her disconsolate text,
Rebelled not, loathing from the trodden heart
    That thing which she had found man's love
      to be.

Dante Gabriel Rossetti

from The Picture of Dorian Gray

'Tell me more about Mr. Dorian Gray. How often do you see him?'

'Every day. I couldn't be happy if I didn't see him every day. He is absolutely necessary to me.'

'How extraordinary! I thought you would never care for anything but your art.'

'He is all my art to me now,' said the painter, gravely. 'I sometimes think, Harry, that there are only two eras of any importance in the world's history. The first is the appearance of a new medium for art, and the second is the appearance of a new personality for art also. What the invention of oil-painting was to the Venetians, the face of Antinoüs was to late Greek sculpture, and the face of Dorian Gray will some day be to me. It is not merely that I paint from him, draw from him, sketch from him. Of course, I have done all that. But he is much more to me than a model or a sitter. I won't tell you that I am dissatisfied with what I have done of him, or that his beauty is such that Art cannot express it. There is nothing that Art cannot express, and I know that the work I have done, since I met Dorian Gray, is good work, is the best work of my life. But in some curious way – I wonder will you understand me? – his personality has suggested to me an entirely new manner in art, an entirely new mode of style. I see things differently, I think of them differently. I can now recreate life in a way that was hidden from me before. "A dream of form in days of thought:" – who is it who says that? I forget; but it is what Dorian Gray has been to me. The merely visible presence of this lad – for he seems to me little more than a lad, though he is really over twenty – his merely visible presence – ah! I wonder can you realise all that that means? Unconsciously he defines for me the lines of a fresh school, a school that is to have in it all the passion of the romantic spirit, all the perfection of the spirit that is Greek. The harmony of soul and body—how much that is! We in our madness have separated the two, and have invented a realism that is vulgar, an ideality that is void. Harry! if you only knew what Dorian Gray is to me! You remember that landscape of mine, for which Agnew offered me such a huge price but which I would not part with? It is one of the best things I have ever done. And why is it so? Because, while I was painting it, Dorian Gray sat beside me. Some subtle influence passed from him to me, and for the first time in my life I saw in the plain woodland the wonder I had always looked for, and always missed.'

'Basil, this is extraordinary! I must see Dorian Gray.'

Hallward got up from the seat, and walked up and down the garden. After some time he came back. 'Harry,' he said, 'Dorian Gray is to me simply a motive in art. You might see nothing in him. I see everything in him. He is never more present in my work than when no image of him is there. He is a suggestion, as I have said, of a new manner. I find him in the curves of certain lines, in the loveliness and subtleties of certain colours. That is all.'

Oscar Wilde

from Great Expectations

'You are part of my existence, part of myself. You have been in every line I have ever read, since I first came here, the rough common boy whose poor heart you wounded even then. You have been in every prospect I have ever seen since – on the river, on the sails of the ships, on the marshes, in the clouds, in the light, in the darkness, in the wind, in the woods, in the sea, in the streets. You have been the embodiment of every graceful fancy that my mind has ever become acquainted with. The stones of which the strongest London buildings are made, are not more real, or more impossible to be displaced by your hands, than your presence and influence have been to me, there and everywhere, and will be. Estella, to the last hour of my life, you cannot choose but remain part of my character, part of the little good in me, part of the evil. But, in this separation I associate you only with the good, and I will faithfully hold you to that always, for you must have done me far more good than harm, let me feel now what sharp distress I may.

Charles Dickens

from Prometheus Unbound

Life of Life! thy lips enkindle
  With their love the breath between them;
And thy smiles before they dwindle
  Make the cold air fire; then screen them
In those looks, where whoso gazes
Faints, entangled in their mazes.

Child of Light! thy limbs are burning
  Through the vest which seems to hide them;
As the radiant lines of morning
  Through thin clouds ere they divide them;
And this atmosphere divinest
Shrouds thee wheresoe'er thou shinest.

Fair are others; none beholds thee;
  But thy voice sounds low and tender
Like the fairest, for it folds thee
  From the sight, that liquid splendour,
And all feel, yet see thee never,
As I feel now, lost for ever!

Lamp of Earth! where'er thou movest
  Its dim shapes are clad with brightness,
And the souls of whom thou lovest
  Walk upon the winds with lightness,
Till they fail, as I am failing,
Dizzy, lost, yet unbewailing!

Percy Bysshe Shelley

The Sick Rose

O rose, thou art sick!
The invisible worm,
That flies in the night,
In the howling storm,

Has found out thy bed
Of crimson joy,
And his dark secret love
Does thy life destroy.

William Blake

from The Count of Monte Cristo

"Countess," returned Franz, totally unheeding her raillery, "I asked you a short time since if you knew any particulars respecting the Albanian lady opposite; I must now beseech you to inform me who and what is her husband?"

"Nay," answered the countess, "I know no more of him than yourself."

"Perhaps you never before noticed him?"

"What a question—so truly French! Do you not know that we Italians have eyes only for the man we love?"

"True," replied Franz.

"All I can say is," continued the countess, taking up the *lorgnette*, and directing it toward the box in question, "that he looks more like a corpse permitted by some friendly grave-digger to quit his tomb for a while, and revisit this earth of ours, than anything human. How ghastly pale he is!"

"Oh, he is always as colorless as you now see him," said Franz.

"Then you know him?" almost screamed the countess. "Oh, pray do, for heaven's sake, tell us all about—is he a vampire, or a resuscitated corpse, or what?"

"I fancy I have seen him before; and I even think he recognizes me."

"And I can well understand," said the countess, shrugging up her beautiful shoulders, as though an involuntary shudder passed through her veins, "that those who have once seen that man will never be likely to forget him."

Alexandre Dumas

from The Lady of Shalott

In the stormy east-wind straining,
The pale yellow woods were waning,
The broad stream in his banks complaining,
Heavily the low sky raining
  Over tower'd Camelot;
Outside the isle a shallow boat
Beneath a willow lay afloat,
Below the carven stern she wrote,
  The Lady of Shalott.

A cloudwhite crown of pearl she dight,
All raimented in snowy white
That loosely flew (her zone in sight
Clasp'd with one blinding diamond bright)
  Her wide eyes fix'd on Camelot,
Though the squally east-wind keenly
Blew, with folded arms serenely
By the water stood the queenly
  Lady of Shalott.

With a steady stony glance—
Like some bold seer in a trance,
Beholding all his own mischance,

Mute, with a glassy countenance—
   She look'd down to Camelot.
It was the closing of the day:
She loos'd the chain, and down she lay;
The broad stream bore her far away,
   The Lady of Shalott.

As when to sailors while they roam,
By creeks and outfalls far from home,
Rising and dropping with the foam,
From dying swans wild warblings come,
   Blown shoreward; so to Camelot
Still as the boathead wound along
The willowy hills and fields among,
They heard her chanting her deathsong,
   The Lady of Shalott.

A longdrawn carol, mournful, holy,
She chanted loudly, chanted lowly,
Till her eyes were darken'd wholly,
And her smooth face sharpen'd slowly,
   Turn'd to tower'd Camelot:
For ere she reach'd upon the tide
The first house by the water-side,

Singing in her song she died,
    The Lady of Shalott.

Under tower and balcony,
By garden wall and gallery,
A pale, pale corpse she floated by,
Deadcold, between the houses high,
    Dead into tower'd Camelot.
Knight and burgher, lord and dame,
To the planked wharfage came:
Below the stern they read her name,
    The Lady of Shalott.

They cross'd themselves, their stars they blest,
Knight, minstrel, abbot, squire, and guest.
There lay a parchment on her breast,
That puzzled more than all the rest,
    The wellfed wits at Camelot.
'The web was woven curiously,
The charm is broken utterly,
Draw near and fear not,—this is I,
    The Lady of Shalott.'

Alfred, Lord Tennyson

THE LINE OF BEAUTY

The Line of Beauty

When mountains crumble and rivers all run dry,
    When every flower has fallen and summer
      fails
    To come again, when the sun's splendour
      pales,
And earth with lagging footsteps seems well-nigh
Spent in her annual circuit through the sky;
    When love is a quenched flame, and nought
      avails
    To save decrepit man, who feebly wails
And lies down lost in the great grave to die;
What is eternal? What escapes decay?
    A certain faultless, matchless, deathless line,
    Curving consummate. Death, Eternity,
Add nought to it, from it take nought away;
    'Twas all God's gift and all man's mastery
    God become human and man grown divine.

Arthur O'Shaughnessy

from Hamlet
Act 4 scene 7

QUEEN

There is a willow grows aslant a brook,
That shows his hoar leaves in the glassy
  stream;
There with fantastic garlands did she come
Of crow-flowers, nettles, daisies, and long
  purples
That liberal shepherds give a grosser name,
But our cold maids do dead men's fingers
  call them:
There, on the pendent boughs her coronet
  weeds
Clambering to hang, an envious sliver broke;
When down her weedy trophies and herself
Fell in the weeping brook. Her clothes spread
  wide;
And, mermaid-like, awhile they bore her up;
Which time she chanted snatches of old
  tunes,
As one incapable of her own distress,
Or like a creature native and indued
Unto that element: but long it could not be

Till that her garments, heavy with their drink,
Pull'd the poor wretch from her melodious lay
To muddy death.

William Shakespeare

Separated

Do not write. I am sad, and want my light put
  out.
Summers in your absence are as dark as a room.
I have closed my arms again. They must do
  without.
To knock at my heart is like knocking at a tomb.
    Do not write!

Do not write. Let us learn to die, as best we may.
Did I love you? Ask God. Ask yourself. Do you
  know?
To hear that you love me, when you are far away,
Is like hearing from heaven and never to go.
    Do not write!

Do not write. I fear you. I fear to remember,
For memory holds the voice I have often heard.
To the one who cannot drink, do not show
  water,
The beloved one's picture in the handwritten
  word.
    Do not write!

Do not write those gentle words that I dare not
    see,
It seems that your voice is spreading them on
    my heart,
Across your smile, on fire, they appear to me,
It seems that a kiss is printing them on my heart.
        Do not write!

Marceline Desbordes-Valmore

from The Woman in White

Where is the woman who has ever really torn from her heart the image that has been once fixed in it by a true love? Books tell us that such unearthly creatures have existed – but what does our own experience say in answer to books?

Wilkie Collins

A DREAM OF DEATH

A Dream of Death

I dreamed that one had died in a strange place
Near no accustomed hand;
And they had nailed the boards above her face,
The peasants of that land,
Wondering to lay her in that solitude,
And raised above her mound
A cross they had made out of two bits of wood
And planted cypress round;
And left her to the indifferent stars above
Until I carved these words:
She was more beautiful than thy first love,
But now lies under boards.

                                          W. B. Yeats

Death and the Lady

DEATH.

Lady, lady, come with me,
I am thy true friend;
New and strange sights shalt thou see
If thine hand thou'lt lend.

LADY.

Wo is me, what dost thou here?
Spectre foul, away!
No more let me those accents hear
Which fill me with dismay.

DEATH.

Thou shalt lie in my arms to-night;
My bed is narrow and cold;
When morning dawns there is no light,
For its curtains are made of mould.

LADY.

Ah, me! ah, me! what's that you say?
And what the bed you mean?
Ah! if I dream, God send it day,
And drive you from mine eyne!

DEATH.

Lady, lady, it must not be;
Look on me once again;
In different shapes you oft see me,
The friend of grief and pain.

LADY.

Oh! sure I once have look'd on thee,
Thy vest is snowy white;
Tall is thy form, I did it see
By yonder pale moonlight.

The mortal lay in a silken bed
Of bright and gaudy hue,
On a pillow of down repos'd her head,
Bound with a fillet of blue.

The tall sprite now her bed drew near,
And stretch'd the curtains wide;
The mortal glanc'd in trembling fear,
But swift her face did hide.

For his robe of mist no more conceal'd
His skeleton form from view,

Each white rib was to sight reveal'd,
And his eyeless sockets too.

Tall and lank, and sadly gaunt,
His rueful form was seen,
His grisly ribs no flesh could vaunt,
Misty the space between.

DEATH.

Lady, fresh and fair there are,
Young and blooming too;
Fate, nor fresh nor young will spare,
Nor now can favour you.

LADY.

Not in my prime? Oh! say not so;
Fair the morn will be,
Gaily rise when I am low,
The sun no more to see.

DEATH.

Hast thou not seen the sun, I pray,
Full many a time before?
Hast thou not curs'd the tardy day,
And wept till it was o'er?

LADY.

Alas! I thought not what I said:
Oh, Death, in pity spare!
Let me not with thee be laid
While I am young and fair.

DEATH.

What hast thou known but care and sorrow?
Thy lovers faithless all?
And if I spare thee till to-morrow
Some horrid ill may fall.

LADY.

'Tis true no peace I've ever known,
My days have pass'd in woe
I trust, since those in grief have gone,
The rest will not thus go.

DEATH.

Deceitful hope! to-morrow's dawn
A dire mishap shall bring;
From my dim shades I come to warn—
Thy friend as well as King.

LADY.
Ah, yet awhile, ah, yet awhile,
This ill I do not fear;
By care I may its course beguile,
But why com'st thou so near?

DEATH
Mortal wretched, mortal vain!
Child of weakest woe!
Sickness, sorrow, tears, and pain
Are all you e'er can know.

Say, what in life is there to lure
Thy agitated mind?
Trifling, futile, vain, unsure—
Oh, wherefore art thou blind?

Thou dost not live e'en half thy day,
For part is spent in tears;
In sleep how much is worn away!
How much in hopes and fears!

In doubt you move, in doubt you live,
Surrounded by a cloud;

Nor up can pierce, nor downward dive,
And yet of life are proud.

Danger, danger lurks around,
False is the smile of man;
Unsteady is the sinking ground,
Delusions croud thy span.

Is there a bliss you e'er can feel
Your million woes to pay?
Is there a day which fails to steal
Some transient joy away?

Is there a beam, which gilds thy morn
With radiance falsely bright,
That sinks not in the evening storm
Which crushes thee ere night?

Life is a bitter, bitter hour,
A bleak, a dreary wild,
Where blooms no shrub, where blows no flow'r
For nature's wretched child.

If from the grave to look on life
With retrospective eye

We sad could view its noisy strife,
Who would not wish to die?

A fev'rish dream, a bubble frail,
Borne on inconstant air.
The bubble bursts—there's none bewail,
For thousands still are there!

No trace remains—the world goes on
As tho' thou ne'er hadst been;
Thou griev'st to die, others grieve none,
Nor miss thee from the scene.

A speck in nature's vast profound,
Unknown thy life or birth—
Giddily flying in the round,
Then add a grain to earth.

Mortal wretched, mortal vain,
Longer wilt thou stay?
Longer wilt thou suffer pain,
Or cheat the coming day?

And then the spectre heav'd a sigh,
A sigh both long and deep,

In mist his changeful form drew nigh,
And he saw the mortal weep.

Then far, far off 'twas seen to glide,
Shrouded in vapours blue;
Small, small it seem'd, but did not hide,
Then gradual rose to view.

With dazzling light the chamber shone,
And tall the sprite appear'd,
And when the solemn bell toll'd one,
The lady no longer fear'd.

"Come quit thy bed, fair lady, I say,
For mine, which is narrow and cold;
When morning dawns there is no day,
For its curtains are made of mould.

"But I'll give thee a robe of vapors blue,
Nor laces nor silks have I;
I'll gem thy brows with a fillet of dew,
Which lasts but while you die.

"And I'll give you to her from whom you came,
Your bed shall be peaceful and lone;

Your mother's cold arms will embrace you again,
And your covering shall be stone.

"There no more griefs shall ever you know,
Nor day nor night shall you see;
Secure in your narrow bed below,
Companion true to me."

"God pardon me," the lady cried,
"And receive me to thy feet,
And all that pure and holy died,
Oh! grant that I may meet."

Then rising from her silken bed,
She gave her hand to Death;
His touch'd, benumb'd, her soul with dread,
And stopp'd her rising breath.

Charlotte Dacre

Because I could not stop for Death

Because I could not stop for Death –
He kindly stopped for me –
The Carriage held but just Ourselves –
And Immortality.

We slowly drove – He knew no haste
And I had put away
My labor and my leisure too,
For His Civility –

We passed the School, where Children strove
At Recess – in the Ring –
We passed the Fields of Gazing Grain –
We passed the Setting Sun –

Or rather – He passcd Us –
The Dews drew quivering and Chill –
For only Gossamer, my Gown –
My Tippet – only Tulle –

We paused before a House that seemed
A Swelling of the Ground –
The Roof was scarcely visible –
The Cornice – in the Ground –

Since then – 'tis Centuries – and yet
Feels shorter than the Day
I first surmised the Horses' Heads
Were toward Eternity –

Emily Dickinson

from Wuthering Heights

'May she wake in torment!' he cried, with frightful vehemence, stamping his foot, and groaning in a sudden paroxysm of ungovernable passion. 'Why, she's a liar to the end! Where is she? Not *there* – not in heaven – not perished – where? Oh! you said you cared nothing for my sufferings! And I pray one prayer – I repeat it till my tongue stiffens – Catherine Earnshaw, may you not rest as long as I am living! You said I killed you – haunt me, then! The murdered *do* haunt their murderers. I believe – I know that ghosts *have* wandered on earth. Be with me always – take any form – drive me mad! Only *do* not leave me in this abyss, where I cannot find you! Oh, God! It is unutterable! I *cannot* live without my life! I *cannot* live without my soul!'

Emily Brontë

The Poor Ghost

'Oh whence do you come, my dear friend,
  to me,
With your golden hair all fallen below your
  knee,
And your face as white as snowdrops on
  the lea,
And your voice as hollow as the hollow sea?'

'From the other world I come back to you:
My locks are uncurled with dripping drenching
  dew,
You know the old, whilst I know the new:
But to-morrow you shall know this too.'

'Oh not to-morrow into the dark, I pray;
Oh not to-morrow, too soon to go away:
Here I feel warm and well-content and gay:
Give me another year, another day.'

'Am I so changed in a day and a night
That mine own only love shrinks from me with
  fright,

Is fain to turn away to left or right
And cover up his eyes from the sight?'

'Indeed I loved you, my chosen friend,
I loved you for life, but life has an end;
Through sickness I was ready to tend:
But death mars all, which we cannot mend.

'Indeed I loved you; I love you yet,
If you will stay where your bed is set,
Where I have planted a violet,
Which the wind waves, which the dew makes
    wet.'

'Life is gone, then love too is gone,
It was a reed that I leant upon:
Never doubt I will leave you alone
And not wake you rattling bone with bone.

'I go home alone to my bed,
Dug deep at the foot and deep at the head,
Roofed in with a load of lead,
Warm enough for the forgotten dead.

'But why did your tears soak through the clay,
And why did your sobs wake me where I lay?
I was away, far enough away:
Let me sleep now till the Judgment Day.'

Christina Rossetti

La Belle Dame sans Merci: A Ballad

I

O what can ail thee, knight-at-arms,
  Alone and palely loitering?
The sedge has withered from the lake,
  And no birds sing.

II

O what can ail thee, knight-at-arms,
  So haggard and so woe-begone?
The squirrel's granary is full,
  And the harvest's done.

III

I see a lily on thy brow,
  With anguish moist and fever-dew,
And on thy cheeks a fading rose
  Fast withereth too.

IV

I met a lady in the meads,
  Full beautiful – a faery's child,
Her hair was long, her foot was light,
  And her eyes were wild.

V

I made a garland for her head,
    And bracelets too, and fragrant zone;
She looked at me as she did love,
    And made sweet moan.

VI

I set her on my pacing steed,
    And nothing else saw all day long,
For sidelong would she bend, and sing
    A faery's song.

VII

She found me roots of relish sweet,
    And honey wild, and manna-dew,
And sure in language strange she said –
    'I love thee true'.

VIII

She took me to her elfin grot,
    And there she wept and sighed full sore,
And there I shut her wild wild eyes
    With kisses four.

IX

And there she lullèd me asleep
  And there I dreamed – Ah! woe betide! –
The latest dream I ever dreamt
  On the cold hill side.

X

I saw pale kings and princes too,
  Pale warriors, death-pale were they all;
They cried – 'La Belle Dame sans Merci
  Hath thee in thrall!'

XI

I saw their starved lips in the gloam,
  With horrid warning gapèd wide,
And I awoke and found me here,
  On the cold hill's side.

XII

And this is why I sojourn here,
  Alone and palely loitering,
Though the sedge is withered from the lake,
  And no birds sing.

John Keats

Annabel Lee

It was many and many a year ago,
　　In a kingdom by the sea,
That a maiden there lived whom you may know
　　By the name of Annabel Lee;
And this maiden she lived with no other thought
　　Than to love and be loved by me.

I was a child and *she* was a child,
　　In this kingdom by the sea,
But we loved with a love that was more than love—
　　I and my Annabel Lee—
With a love that the wingèd seraphs of Heaven
　　Coveted her and me.

And this was the reason that, long ago,
　　In this kingdom by the sea,
A wind blew out of a cloud, chilling
　　My beautiful Annabel Lee;
So that her highborn kinsmen came
　　And bore her away from me,
To shut her up in a sepulchre
　　In this kingdom by the sea.

The angels, not half so happy in Heaven,
    Went envying her and me—
Yes!—that was the reason (as all men know,
    In this kingdom by the sea)
That the wind came out of the cloud by night,
    Chilling and killing my Annabel Lee.

But our love it was stronger by far than the love
    Of those who were older than we—
    Of many far wiser than we—
And neither the angels in Heaven above
    Nor the demons down under the sea
Can ever dissever my soul from the soul
    Of the beautiful Annabel Lee;

For the moon never beams, without bringing
  me dreams
    Of the beautiful Annabel Lee;
And the stars never rise, but I feel the bright
  eyes
    Of the beautiful Annabel Lee;
And so, all the night-tide, I lie down by the side

Of my darling—my darling—my life and
  my bride,
In her sepulchre there by the sea—
In her tomb by the sounding sea.

Edgar Allan Poe

from Doctor Faustus

O half the hour is passed! 'Twill all be passed
  anon!
O God,
If thou wilt not have mercy on my soul,
Yet for Christ's sake, whose blood hath
  ransomed me,
Impose some end to my incessant pain!
Let Faustus live in hell a thousand years,
A hundred thousand, and at last be saved!
No end is limited to damned souls!
Why wert thou not a creature wanting soul?
Or why is this immortal that thou hast?
O, Pythagoras' metempsychosis, were that true,
This soul should fly from me and I be changed
Into some brutish beast.
All beasts are happy, for when they die
Their souls are soon dissolved in elements,
But mine must live still to be plagued in hell!
Cursed be the parents that engendered me!
No, Faustus, curse thyself, curse Lucifer
That hath deprived thee of the joys of heaven.
                        The clock strikes twelve.
It strikes, it strikes! Now body, turn to air,

Or Lucifer will bear thee quick to hell!
O soul, be changed into small water-drops,
And fall into the ocean, ne'er be found.

Christopher Marlowe

I have dreamed of Death

I have dreamed of Death: – what will it be to die
    Not in a dream, but in the literal truth
    With all Death's adjuncts ghastly and
        uncouth,
The pang that is the last and the last sigh?
Too dulled, it may be, for a last good-bye
    Too comfortless for any one to soothe,
    A helpless charmless spectacle of truth

Through long last hours, so long while yet they
  fly.
So long to those who hopeless in their fear
    Watch the slow breath and look for what
        they dread:
While I supine with ears that cease to hear,
    With eyes that glaze, with heart pulse
        running down
(Alas! no saint rejoicing on her bed),
    May miss the goal at last, may miss a
        crown.

Christina Rossetti

Severed Selves

Two separate divided silences,
  Which, brought together, would find loving
    voice;
  Two glances which together would rejoice
In love, now lost like stars beyond dark trees;
Two hands apart whose touch alone gives ease;
    Two bosoms which, heart-shrined with
      mutual flame,
      Would, meeting in one clasp, be made the
      same;
Two souls, the shores wave-mocked of sundering
  seas: –

Such are we now. Ah! may our hope forecast
    Indeed one hour again, when on this stream
    Of darkened love once more the light shall
      gleam? –
An hour how slow to come, how quickly past, –
Which blooms and fades, and only leaves at last,
  Faint as shed flowers, the attenuated dream.

Dante Gabriel Rossetti

The End

If I could have put you in my heart,
If but I could have wrapped you in myself
How glad I should have been!
And now the chart
Of memory unrolls again to me
The course of our journey here, here where we
    part.

And oh, that you had never, never been
Some of your selves, my love; that some
Of your several faces I had never seen!
And still they come before me, and they go;
And I cry aloud in the moments that intervene.

And oh, my love, as I rock for you to-night,
And have not any longer any hope
To heal the suffering, or to make requite
For all your life of asking and despair,
I own that some of me is dead to-night.

D. H. Lawrence

In the Night

Cruel? I think there never was a cheating
More cruel, thro' all the weary days than this!
This is no dream, my heart kept on repeating,
But sober certainty of waking bliss.

Dreams? O, I know their faces – goodly seeming,
Vaporous, whirled on many-coloured wings;
I have had dreams before, this is no dreaming,
But daylight gladness that the daylight brings.

What ails my love; what ails her? She is paling;
Faint grows her face, and slowly seems to fade!
I cannot clasp her – stretch out unavailing
My arms across the silence and the shade.

Amy Levy

Posthumous Remorse

When you go to sleep, my gloomy beauty, below a black marble monument, when from alcove and manor you are reduced to damp vault and hollow grave;

when the stone—pressing on your timorous chest and sides already lulled by a charmed indifference—halts your heart from beating, from willing, your feet from their bold adventuring,

then the tomb, confidant to my infinite dream (since the tomb understands the poet always), through those long nights in which slumber is banished,

will say to you: "What does it profit you, imperfect courtisan, not to have known what the dead weep for?"—And the worm will gnaw at your hide like remorse.

Charles Baudelaire

FAR SAFER, OF A MIDNIGHT,
MEETING EXTERNAL GHOST

One Need Not be a Chamber
to be Haunted

One need not be a chamber – to be Haunted –
One need not be a House –
The Brain – has Corridors surpassing
Material Place –

Far safer, of a Midnight – meeting
External Ghost –
Than an Interior – confronting –
That cooler – Host –

Far safer, through an Abbey – gallop –
The Stones a'chase –
Than moonless – One's A'self encounter –
In lonesome place –

Ourself – behind Ourself – Concealed –
Should startle – most –
Assassin – hid in Our Apartment –
Be Horror's least –

The Prudent – carries a Revolver –
He bolts the Door,
O'erlooking a Superior Spectre
More near –

Emily Dickinson

from Northanger Abbey

'And are you prepared to encounter all the horrors that a building such as "what one reads about" may produce? Have you a stout heart? Nerves fit for sliding panels and tapestry?'

'Oh! yes – I do not think I should be easily frightened, because there would be so many people in the house – and besides, it has never been uninhabited and left deserted for years, and then the family come back to it unawares, without giving any notice, as generally happens.'

'No, certainly. We shall not have to explore our way into a hall dimly lighted by the expiring embers of a wood fire – nor be obliged to spread our beds on the floor of a room without windows, doors, or furniture. But you must be aware that when a young lady is (by whatever means) introduced into a dwelling of this kind, she is always lodged apart from the rest of the family. While they snugly repair to their own end of the house, she is formally conducted by Dorothy, the ancient housekeeper, up a different staircase, and along many gloomy passages, into an apartment never used since some cousin or kin died in it about twenty years before. Can you stand such a ceremony as this? Will not your mind misgive you when you find yourself in this gloomy chamber – too lofty and extensive for you, with only the feeble rays of a single lamp to take in its size – its walls hung with tapestry exhibiting figures as large as life, and the bed, of dark green stuff or purple velvet, presenting even a funereal appearance? Will not your heart sink within you?'

'Oh! But this will not happen to me, I am sure.'

'How fearfully will you examine the furniture of your apartment! And what will you discern? Not tables, toilettes, wardrobes, or drawers, but on one side perhaps the remains of a broken lute, on the other a ponderous chest which no efforts can open, and over the fireplace the portrait of some handsome warrior, whose features will so incomprehensibly strike you, that you will not be able to withdraw your eyes from it. Dorothy meanwhile, no less struck by your appearance, gazes on you in great agitation, and drops a few unintelligible hints. To raise your spirits, moreover, she gives you reason to suppose that the part of the abbey you inhabit is undoubtedly haunted, and informs you that you will not have a single domestic within call. With this parting cordial she curtsies off – you listen to the sound of her receding footsteps as long as the last echo can reach you – and when, with fainting spirits, you attempt to fasten your door, you discover, with increased alarm, that it has no lock.'

'Oh! Mr. Tilney, how frightful! This is just like a book! But it cannot really happen to me. I am sure your housekeeper is not really Dorothy. Well, what then?'

'Nothing further to alarm perhaps may occur the first night. After surmounting your *unconquerable* horror of the bed, you will retire to rest, and get a few hours' unquiet slumber. But on the second, or at farthest the *third* night after your arrival, you will probably have a violent storm. Peals of thunder so loud as to seem to shake the edifice to its foundation will roll round the neighbouring mountains – and during the frightful gusts of wind which accompany it, you will probably think you discern (for your lamp is not extinguished) one part of the hanging more violently agitated than the rest. Unable of course to repress your curiosity in so favourable a moment for indulging it, you will instantly arise, and throwing your dressing-gown around you, proceed to examine this mystery. After a very short search, you will discover a division in the tapestry so artfully constructed as to defy the minutest inspection, and on opening it, a door will immediately appear – which door, being only secured by massy bars and a padlock, you will, after a few efforts, succeed in opening – and, with your lamp in your hand, will pass through it into a small vaulted room.'

'No, indeed; I should be too much frightened to do any such thing.'

'What! Not when Dorothy has given you to understand that there is a secret subterraneous communication between your apartment and the chapel of St Anthony, scarcely two miles off? Could you shrink from so simple an adventure? No, no, you will proceed into this small vaulted room, and through this into several others, without perceiving anything very remarkable in either. In one perhaps there may be a dagger, in another a few drops of blood, and in a third the remains of some instrument of torture; but there being nothing in all this out of the common way, and your lamp being nearly exhausted, you will return towards your own apartment. In repassing through the small vaulted room, however, your eyes will be attracted towards a large, old-fashioned cabinet of ebony and gold, which, though narrowly examining the furniture before, you had passed unnoticed. Impelled by an irresistible presentiment, you will eagerly advance to it, unlock its folding doors, and search into every drawer – but for some time without discovering anything of importance – perhaps nothing but a considerable hoard of diamonds. At last, however, by touching a secret spring, an inner compartment will open – a roll of paper appears – you seize it – it contains many sheets of manuscript – you hasten with the precious treasure into your own chamber, but scarcely have you been able to decipher "Oh! Thou – whomsoever thou mayst be, into whose hands these memoirs of the wretched Matilda may fall" – when your lamp suddenly expires in the socket, and leaves you in total darkness.'

Jane Austen

from The Turn of the Screw

'No, no – there are depths, depths! The more I
go over it the more I see in it, and the more I see
in it the more I fear. I don't know what I *don't*
see – what I *don't* fear!'

Mrs Grose tried to keep up with me. 'You
mean you're afraid of seeing her again?'

'Oh, no; that's nothing – now!' Then I
explained. 'It's of *not* seeing her.'

Henry James

Song of a Mad Girl, Whose Lover Has Died at Sea

Under the green white blue of this and that and
   the other,
That and the other, and that and the other, for
   ever and ever,
Under the up and down and the swaying ships
   swing-swonging,
There they flung him to sleep who will never
   come back to my longing.
The Father comes back to his child and the son
   comes back to his Mother,
But neither by land or sea
Will he ever come back to me,
Never, never, never
Will he come back to me.
All day I run by the Cliff, all night I stand in
   the sand,
All day I furrow and burrow the holmes and
   the heights.
But whether by night or day
There's never a trace or a track,
Never a word or a breath,

In the swill and the swoop and the flash and
     the foam and the wind,
Never a fleck or a speck
Coming, coming my way.
The mew comes back to the strand and the
     ship comes back to the land,
But he will never come back
To all the prayers that I pray thro' the scorching
     black of the day
And the freezing black of the nights,
Never, never come back
To the ear that harks itself deaf and the eye that
     strains itself blind,
And the heart that is starving to death.
He was chill and they threw him to cold,
He was dead and they threw him to drown,
He was weary and wanted rest –
They should have laid him on my breast,
He would have slept on my breast,
But they threw him into the boiling boil and
     bubble,
The wheel and the whirl, the driff and the draff
Of the everlasting trouble.
I swear to you he was mine! I swear to you he
     was my own.

Madam, if I may make so bold,
Do you know what the dead men do
In the black and blue, in the green and brown?
Deep, deep, you think they sleep
Where the mermen moan and the mermaids
  weep?
Ah, ah, you make me laugh!
I'm not yet twenty years old,
But lean your ear
And you shall hear
A little thing that I know.
Up and up they come to the top,
Down and down they go down.
To and fro the finny fish go,
But slow and slow, and so and so,
Low over high, high under low,
Up and up they come to the top,
Down and down they go down:
When the sun comes up they come to the top,
When the sun sinks they go down.

Sydney Dobell

Echo

Come to me in the silence of the night;
   Come in the speaking silence of a dream;
Come with soft rounded cheeks and eyes as bright
    As sunlight on a stream;
    Come back in tears,
O memory, hope, love of finished years.

Oh dream how sweet, too sweet, too bitter sweet
    Whose wakening should have been in
      Paradise,
Where souls brimfull of love abide and meet;
    Where thirsting longing eyes
    Watch the slow door
That opening, letting in, lets out no more.

Yet come to me in dreams, that I may live
    My very life again though cold in death:
Come back to me in dreams, that I may give
    Pulse for pulse, breath for breath:
    Speak low, lean low,
As long ago, my love, how long ago.

Christina Rossetti

Remembrance

Cold in the earth—and the deep snow piled
  above thee,
Far, far removed, cold in the dreary grave!
Have I forgot, my only Love, to love thee,
Severed at last by Time's all-severing wave?

Now, when alone, do my thoughts no longer
  hover
Over the mountains, on that northern shore,
Resting their wings where heath and fern-leaves
  cover
Thy noble heart forever, ever more?

Cold in the earth—and fifteen wild Decembers,
From those brown hills, have melted into spring:
Faithful, indeed, is the spirit that remembers
After such years of change and suffering!

Sweet Love of youth, forgive, if I forget thee,
While the world's tide is bearing me along;
Other desires and other hopes beset me,
Hopes which obscure, but cannot do thee
  wrong!

No later light has lightened up my heaven,
No second morn has ever shone for me;
All my life's bliss from thy dear life was given,
All my life's bliss is in the grave with thee.

But, when the days of golden dreams had
    perished,
And even Despair was powerless to destroy,
Then did I learn how existence could be
    cherished,
Strengthened, and fed without the aid of joy.

Then did I check the tears of useless passion—
Weaned my young soul from yearning after
    thine;
Sternly denied its burning wish to hasten
Down to that tomb already more than mine.

And, even yet, I dare not let it languish,
Dare not indulge in memory's rapturous pain;
Once drinking deep of that divinest anguish,
How could I seek the empty world again?

Emily Brontë

from Frankenstein

There is something at work in my soul which I
do not understand.

Mary Shelley

from Christabel

Is the night chilly and dark?
The night is chilly, but not dark.
The thin gray cloud is spread on high,
It covers but not hides the sky.
The moon is behind, and at the full;
And yet she looks both small and dull.
The night is chill, the cloud is gray:
'Tis a month before the month of May,
And the Spring comes slowly up this way.

The lovely lady, Christabel,
Whom her father loves so well,
What makes her in the wood so late,
A furlong from the castle gate?
She had dreams all yesternight
Of her own betrothèd knight;
And she in the midnight wood will pray
For the weal of her lover that's far away.

She stole along, she nothing spoke,
The sighs she heaved were soft and low,
And naught was green upon the oak
But moss and rarest misletoe:

She kneels beneath the huge oak tree,
And in silence prayeth she.

The lady sprang up suddenly,
The lovely lady Christabel!
It moaned as near, as near can be,
But what it is she cannot tell. —
On the other side it seems to be,
Of the huge, broad-breasted, old oak tree.

The night is chill; the forest bare;
Is it the wind that moaneth bleak?
There is not wind enough in the air
To move away the ringlet curl
From the lovely lady's cheek—
There is not wind enough to twirl
The one red leaf, the last of its clan,
That dances as often as dance it can,
Hanging so light, and hanging so high,
On the topmost twig that looks up at the sky.

Hush, beating heart of Christabel!
Jesu, Maria, shield her well!
She folded her arms beneath her cloak,

And stole to the other side of the oak.
    What sees she there?

There she sees a damsel bright,
Drest in a silken robe of white,
That shadowy in the moonlight shone:
The neck that made that white robe wan,
Her stately neck, and arms were bare;
Her blue-veined feet unsandl'd were,
And wildly glittered here and there
The gems entangled in her hair.
I guess, 'twas frightful there to see
A lady so richly clad as she—
Beautiful exceedingly!

                            Samuel Taylor Coleridge

The Shadow on the Stone

I went by the Druid stone
That broods in the garden white and lone,
And I stopped and looked at the shifting
shadows
That at some moments fall thereon
From the tree hard by with a rhythmic swing,
And they shaped in my imagining
To the shade that a well-known head and
shoulders
Threw there when she was gardening.

I thought her behind my back,
Yea, her I long had learned to lack,
And I said: 'I am sure you are standing
behind me,
Though how do you get into this old track?'
And there was no sound but the fall of a leaf
As a sad response; and to keep down grief
I would not turn my head to discover
That there was nothing in my belief.

Yet I wanted to look and see
That nobody stood at the back of me;

But I thought once more: 'Nay, I'll not unvision
    A shape which, somehow, there may be.'
    So I went on softly from the glade,
    And left her behind me throwing her shade,
As she were indeed an apparition—
    My head unturned lest my dream should
        fade.

Thomas Hardy

from The Affliction of Margaret

XXIV. Bitter Sorrow

I look for ghosts; but none will force
Their way to me: 'tis falsely said
That there was ever intercourse
Between the living and the dead;
For, surely, then I should have sight
Of him I wait for day and night,
With love and longings infinite.

My apprehensions come in crowds,
I dread the rustling of the grass;
The very shadows of the clouds
Have power to shake me as they pass:
I question things and do not find
One that will answer to my mind;
And all the world appears unkind.

Beyond participation lie
My troubles, and beyond relief:
If any chance to heave a sigh,
They pity me, and not my grief.
Then come to me, my Son, or send

Some tidings that my woes may end;
I have no other earthly friend!

William Wordsworth

from The Phantom of the Opera

'She is not herself tonight . . . She is usually so gentle . . .'

Then he said good-night; and Raoul was left alone. The whole of this part of the theatre was now deserted. The farewell ceremony was no doubt taking place in the foyer of the ballet. Raoul thought that Daaé might go to it; and he waited in the silent solitude, even hid himself in the kindly shadow of a doorway. He still felt a terrible pain at his heart; and it was of this that he wished to speak to Daaé without delay.

Suddenly, the dressing-room door opened and the maid came out by herself, carrying bundles. He stopped her and asked how her mistress was. The woman laughed and said that she was quite well, but that he must not disturb her, for she wished to be left alone. And she passed on. A single idea crossed Raoul's burning brain: of course, Daaé wished to be left alone *for him!* Had he not told her that he wanted to speak to her privately?

Hardly breathing, he went up to the dressing-room and, with his ear to the door to catch her reply, prepared to knock. But his hand dropped. He had heard a *man's voice* in the dressing-room, saying, in a curiously masterful tone: 'Christine, you must love me!'

And Christine's voice, infinitely sad and trembling, as though accompanied by tears, replied: 'How can you talk like that? *When I sing only for you? . . .*'

Raoul leant against the panel to ease his pain. His heart, which had seemed gone for ever, returned to his breast and was throbbing loudly. The whole passage echoed with its beating; and Raoul's ears were deafened. Surely, if his heart continued to make such a noise, they would hear it inside, they would open the door and the young man would be turned away in disgrace. What a position for a Chagny! To be caught listening behind a door! He seized his heart in his two hands to make it stop.

The man's voice spoke again: 'Are you very tired?'

'Oh, tonight, I gave you my soul and I am dead!'

'Your soul is a beautiful thing, child,' replied

the man's grave voice, 'and I thank you. No emperor ever received so fair a gift. *The angels wept tonight.*'

Gaston Leroux

THE EARTH IS A TOMB, THE
GAUDY SKY A VAULT, WE BUT
WALKING CORPSES

from On Ghosts

For my own part, I never saw a ghost except once in a dream. I feared it in my sleep; I awoke trembling, and lights and the speech of others could hardly dissipate my fear. Some years ago I lost a friend, and a few months afterwards visited the house where I had last seen him. It was deserted, and though in the midst of a city, its vast halls and spacious apartments occasioned the same sense of loneliness as if it had been situated on an uninhabited heath. I walked through the vacant chambers by twilight, and none save I awakened the echoes of their pavement. The far mountains (visible from the upper windows) had lost their tinge of sunset; the tranquil atmosphere grew leaden coloured as the golden stars appeared in the firmament; no wind ruffled the shrunk-up river which crawled lazily through the deepest channel of its wide and empty bed; the chimes of the Ave Maria had ceased, and the bell hung moveless in the open belfry: beauty invested a reposing world, and awe was inspired by beauty only. I walked through the rooms filled with sensations of the most poignant grief. He had been there; his living frame had been caged by those walls, his breath had mingled with that atmosphere, his step had been on those stones, I thought:—the earth is a tomb, the gaudy sky a vault, we but walking corpses. The wind rising in the east rushed through the open casements, making them shake;—methought, I heard, I felt—I know not what—but I trembled. To have seen him but for a moment, I would have knelt until the stones had been worn by the impress, so I told myself, and so I knew a moment after, but then I trembled, awe-struck and fearful. Wherefore? There is something beyond us of which we are ignorant. The sun drawing up the vaporous air makes a void, and the wind rushes in to fill it,—thus beyond our soul's ken there is an empty space; and our hopes and fears, in gentle gales or terrific whirlwinds, occupy the vacuum; and if it does no more, it bestows on the feeling heart a belief that influences do exist to watch and guard us, though they be impalpable to the coarser faculties.

Mary Shelley

Lady Alice

I

What doth Lady Alice so late on the turret stair,
Without a lamp to light her, but the diamond
  in her hair;
When every arching passage overflows with
  shallow gloom,
And dreams float through the castle, into every
  silent room?

She trembles at her footsteps, although they fall
  so light;
Through the turret loopholes she sees the wild
  mid-night;
Broken vapours streaming across the stormy sky;
Down the empty corridors the blast doth moan
  and cry.

She steals along a gallery; she pauses by a door
And fast her tears are dropping down upon the
  oaken floor;
And thrice she seems returning – but thrice she
  turns again: –

Now heavy lie the cloud of sleep on that old
   father's brain!

Oh, well it were that *never* shouldst thou waken
   from thy sleep!
For wherefore should they waken, who waken
   but to weep?
No more, no more beside thy bed doth Peace a
   vigil keep,
But Woe, – a lion that awaits thy rousing for its
   leap.

II

An afternoon in April, no sun appears on high,
But a moist and yellow lustre fills the deepness
   of the sky:
And through the castle-gateway, left empty and
   forlorn,
Along the leafless avenue an honour'd bier is
   borne.

They stop. The long line closes up like some
   gigantic worm;
A shape is standing in the path, a wan and
   ghost-like form,

Which gazes fixedly; nor moves; nor utters any
  sound;
Then, like a statue built of snow, sinks down
  upon the ground.

And though her clothes are ragged, and though
  her feet are bare,
And though all wild and tangled falls her heavy
  silk-brown hair;
Though from her eyes the brightness, from her
  cheeks the bloom is fled,
They know their Lady Alice, the darling of the
  dead.

With silence, in her own old room the fainting
  form they lay,
Where all things stand unalter'd since the night
  she fled away:
But who – but who shall bring to life her father
  from the clay?
But who shall give her back again her heart of a
  former day?

William Allingham

The Haunted House

'I seem like one
Who treads alone
  Some banquet hall deserted,
Whose lights are fled,
Whose garlands dead,
  And all but me departed.'

Thomas Moore, 'Oft, in the Stilly Night
(Scotch Air)'

See'st thou yon grey gleaming hall,
Where the deep elm-shadows fall?
Voices that have left the earth
  Long ago,
Still are murmuring round its hearth,
  Soft and low:
Ever there; – yet one alone
Hath the gift to hear their tone.
Guests come thither, and depart,
Free of step, and light of heart;
Children, with sweet visions bless'd,
In the haunted chambers rest;
One alone unslumbering lies
When the night hath seal'd all eyes,

One quick heart and watchful ear,
Listening for those whispers clear.

See'st thou where the woodbine flowers
O'er yon low porch hang in showers?
Startling faces of the dead,
   Pale, yet sweet,
One lone woman's entering tread
   There still meet!
Some with young smooth foreheads fair,
Faintly shining through bright hair;
Some with reverend locks of snow –
All, all buried long ago!
All, from under deep sea-waves,
Or the flowers of foreign graves,
Or the old and banner'd aisle,
Where their high tombs gleam the while;
Rising, wandering, floating by,
Suddenly and silently,
Through their earthly home and place,
But amidst another race.

Wherefore, unto one alone,
Are those sounds and visions known?
Wherefore hath that spell of power
    Dark and dread,
On *her* soul, a baleful dower,
    Thus been shed?
Oh! in those deep-seeing eyes,
No strange gift of mystery lies!
She is lone where once she moved,
Fair, and happy, and beloved!
Sunny smiles were glancing round her,
Tendrils of kind hearts had bound her.
Now those silver chords are broken,
Those bright looks have left no token;
Not one trace on all the earth,
Save her memory of their mirth.
She is lone and lingering now,
Dreams have gather'd o'er her brow,
'Midst gay songs and children's play,
She is dwelling far away
Seeing what none else may see –
Haunted still her place must be!

Felicia Dorothea Hemans

from Street Haunting

In these minutes in which a ghost has been sought for, a quarrel composed, and a pencil bought, the streets had become completely empty. Life had withdrawn to the top floor, and lamps were lit. The pavement was dry and hard; the road was of hammered silver. Walking home through the desolation one could tell oneself the story of the dwarf, of the blind men, of the party in the Mayfair mansion, of the quarrel in the stationer's shop. Into each of these lives one could penetrate a little way, far enough to give oneself the illusion that one is not tethered to a single mind, but can put on briefly for a few minutes the bodies and minds of others. One could become a washerwoman, a publican, a street singer. And what greater delight and wonder can there be than to leave the straight lines of personality and deviate into those footpaths that lead beneath brambles and thick tree trunks into the heart of the forest where live those wild beasts, our fellow men?

That is true: to escape is the greatest of pleasures; street haunting in winter the greatest of adventures. Still as we approach our own door-step again, it is comforting to feel the old possessions, the old prejudices, fold us round; and the self, which has been blown about at so many street corners, which has battered like a moth at the flame of so many inaccessible lanterns, sheltered and enclosed. Here again is the usual door; here the chair turned as we left it and the china bowl and the brown ring on the carpet. And here—let us examine it tenderly, let us touch it with reverence—is the only spoil we have retrieved from all the treasures of the city, a lead pencil.

Virginia Woolf

My Ghost

A story told to my little cousin Kate.

Yes, Katie, I think you are very sweet,
Now that the tangles are out of your hair,
And you sing as well as the birds you meet,
That are playing, like you, in the blossoms there.
But now you are coming to kiss me, you say:
Well, what is it for? Shall I tie your shoe,
Or loop your sleeve in a prettier way?
"Do I know about ghosts?" Indeed I do.

"Have I seen one?" Yes: last evening, you know,
We were taking a walk that you had to miss,
(I think you were naughty and cried to go,
But, surely, you'll stay at home after this!)
And, away in the twilight lonesomely
("What is the twilight?" It's—getting late!)
I was thinking of things that were sad to me—
There, hush! you know nothing about them,
    Kate.

Well, we had to go through the rocky lane,
Close to that bridge where the water roars,
By a still, red house, where the dark and rain

Go in when they will at the open doors;
And the moon, that had just waked up, look'd
   through
The broken old windows and seem'd afraid,
And the wild bats flew and the thistles grew
Where once in the roses the children play'd.

Just across the road by the cherry-trees
Some fallen white stones had been lying so long,
Half hid in the grass, and under these
There were people dead. I could hear the song
Of a very sleepy dove, as I pass'd
The graveyard near, and the cricket that cried;
And I look'd (ah! the Ghost is coming at last!)
And something was walking at my side.

It seem'd to be wrapp'd in a great dark shawl,
(For the night was a little cold, you know.)
It would not speak. It was black and tall;
And it walk'd so proudly and very slow.
Then it mock'd me—every thing I could do:
Now it caught at the lightning-flies like me;
Now it stopp'd where the elder-blossoms grew;
Now it tore the thorns from a gray bent tree.

Still it follow'd me under the yellow moon,
Looking back to the graveyard now and then,
Where the winds were playing the night a tune—
But, Kate, a Ghost doesn't care for men,
And your papa couldn't have done it harm!
Ah, dark-eyed darling, what is it you see?
There, you needn't hide in your dimpled arm—
It was only my Shadow that walk'd with me!

Sarah Morgan Bryan Piatt

The Tune of Seven Towers

No one goes there now:
　　For what is left to fetch away
From the desolate battlements all arow,
　　And the lead roof heavy and grey?
'Therefore,' said fair Yoland of the flowers,
'This is the tune of Seven Towers.'

No one walks there now;
　　Except in the white moonlight
The white ghosts walk in a row;
　　If one could see it, an awful sight, –
'Listen!' said fair Yoland of the flowers,
'This is the tune of Seven Towers.'

But none can see them now,
　　Though they sit by the side of the moat,
Feet half in the water, there in a row,
　　Long hair in the wind afloat.
'Therefore,' said fair Yoland of the flowers,
'This is the tune of Seven Towers.'

If any will go to it now,
    He must go to it all alone,
Its gates will not open to any row
    Of glittering spears – will *you* go alone?
'Listen!' said fair Yoland of the flowers,
'This is the tune of Seven Towers.'

By my love go there now,
    To fetch me my coif away,
My coif and my kirtle, with pearls arow,
    Oliver, go to-day!
'Therefore,' said fair Yoland of the flowers,
'This is the tune of Seven Towers.'

I am unhappy now,
    I cannot tell you why;
If you go, the priests and I in a row
    Will pray that you may not die.
'Listen!' said fair Yoland of the flowers,
'This is the tune of Seven Towers.'

If you will go for me now,
    I will kiss your mouth at last;
        [*She sayeth inwardly.*]

(*The graves stand grey in a row,*)
    Oliver, hold me fast!
'Therefore,' said fair Yoland of the flowers,
'This is the tune of Seven Towers.'

William Morris

The Garden of Love

I went to the Garden of Love,
And saw what I never had seen:
A Chapel was built in the midst,
Where I used to play on the green.

And the gates of this Chapel were shut,
And 'Thou shalt not' writ over the door;
So I turn'd to the Garden of Love,
That so many sweet flowers bore.

And I saw it was filled with graves,
And tomb-stones where flowers should be:
And Priests in black gowns, were walking their
    rounds,
And binding with briars, my joys & desires.

William Blake

from Maud

A Monodrama

Come into the garden, Maud,
    For the black bat, night, has flown,
Come into the garden, Maud,
    I am here at the gate alone;
And the woodbine spices are wafted abroad,
    And the musk of the rose is blown.

For a breeze of morning moves,
    And the planet of Love is on high,
Beginning to faint in the light that she loves
    In a bed of daffodil sky,
To faint in the light of the sun she loves,
    To faint in his light, and to die.

All night have the roses heard
    The flute, violin, bassoon;
All night has the casement jessamine stirr'd
    To the dancers dancing in tune;
Till a silence fell with the waking bird,
    And a hush with the setting moon.

I said to the lily, "There is but one
    With whom she has heart to be gay.
When will the dancers leave her alone?
    She is weary of dance and play."
Now half to the setting moon are gone,
    And half to the rising day;
Low on the sand and loud on the stone
    The last wheel echoes away.

I said to the rose, "The brief night goes
    In babble and revel and wine.
O young lord-lover, what sighs are those,
    For one that will never be thine?
But mine, but mine," so I sware to the rose,
    "For ever and ever, mine."

And the soul of the rose went into my blood,
    As the music clash'd in the hall;
And long by the garden lake I stood,
    For I heard your rivulet fall
From the lake to the meadow and on to the wood,
    Our wood, that is dearer than all;

From the meadow your walks have left so sweet
　　That whenever a March-wind sighs
He sets the jewel-print of your feet
　　In violets blue as your eyes,
To the woody hollows in which we meet
　　And the valleys of Paradise.

The slender acacia would not shake
　　One long milk-bloom on the tree;
The white lake-blossom fell into the lake
　　As the pimpernel dozed on the lea;
But the rose was awake all night for your sake,
　　Knowing your promise to me;
The lilies and roses were all awake,
　　They sigh'd for the dawn and thee.

Queen rose of the rosebud garden of girls,
　　Come hither, the dances are done,
In gloss of satin and glimmer of pearls,
　　Queen lily and rose in one;
Shine out, little head, sunning over with curls,
　　To the flowers, and be their sun.

There has fallen a splendid tear
    From the passion-flower at the gate.
She is coming, my dove, my dear;
    She is coming, my life, my fate;
The red rose cries, "She is near, she is near;"
    And the white rose weeps, "She is late;"
The larkspur listens, "I hear, I hear;"
    And the lily whispers, "I wait."

She is coming, my own, my sweet;
    Were it ever so airy a tread,
My heart would hear her and beat,
    Were it earth in an earthy bed;
My dust would hear her and beat,
    Had I lain for a century dead,
Would start and tremble under her feet,
    And blossom in purple and red.

Alfred, Lord Tennyson

Hymn to the Night

Aspasie, trillistos.

I heard the trailing garments of the Night
    Sweep through her marble halls!
I saw her sable skirts all fringed with light
    From the celestial walls!

I felt her presence, by its spell of might,
    Stoop o'er me from above;
The calm, majestic presence of the Night,
    As of the one I love.

I heard the sounds of sorrow and delight,
    The manifold, soft chimes,
That fill the haunted chambers of the Night,
    Like some old poet's rhymes.

From the cool cisterns of the midnight air
    My spirit drank repose;
The fountain of perpetual peace flows there,—
    From those deep cisterns flows.

O holy Night! from thee I learn to bear
    What man has borne before!
Thou layest thy finger on the lips of Care,
    And they complain no more.

Peace! Peace! Orestes-like I breathe this prayer!
    Descend with broad-winged flight,
The welcome, the thrice-prayed for, the most fair,
    The best-beloved Night!

Henry Wadsworth Longfellow

Shadwell Stair

I am the ghost of Shadwell Stair.
  Along the wharves by the water-house,
  And through the cavernous slaughter-house,
I am the shadow that walks there.

Yet I have flesh both firm and cool,
  And eyes tumultuous as the gems
  Of moons and lamps in the full Thames
When dusk sails wavering down the pool.

Shuddering the purple street-arc burns
  Where I watch always; from the banks
  Dolorously the shipping clanks
And after me a strange tide turns.

I walk till the stars of London wane
  And dawn creeps up the Shadwell Stair.
  But when the crowing syrens blare
I with another ghost am lain.

Wilfred Owen

The Eve of St. Agnes

I

St Agnes' Eve – Ah, bitter chill it was!
The owl, for all his feathers, was a-cold;
The hare limped trembling through the
    frozen grass,
And silent was the flock in woolly fold:
Numb were the Beadsman's fingers, while
    he told
His rosary, and while his frosted breath,
Like pious incense from a censer old,
Seemed taking flight for heaven, without a
    death,
Past the sweet Virgin's picture, while his prayer
he saith.

II

His prayer he saith, this patient, holy man;
Then takes his lamp, and riseth from his
    knees,
And back returneth, meagre, barefoot, wan,
Along the chapel aisle by slow degrees:
The sculptured dead, on each side, seem to
    freeze,

Emprisoned in black, purgatorial rails:
Knights, ladies, praying in dumb orat'ries,
He passeth by; and his weak spirit fails
To think how they may ache in icy hoods and
  mails.

III

Northward he turneth through a little door,
And scarce three steps, ere Music's golden
  tongue
Flattered to tears this agèd man and poor;
But no – already had his deathbell rung:
The joys of all his life were said and sung:
His was harsh penance on St Agnes' Eve.
Another way he went, and soon among
Rough ashes sat he for his soul's reprieve,
And all night kept awake, for sinners' sake to
  grieve.

IV

That ancient Beadsman heard the prelude
  soft;
And so it chanced, for many a door was wide,
From hurry to and fro. Soon, up aloft,
The silver, snarling trumpets 'gan to chide:

The level chambers, ready with their pride,
Were glowing to receive a thousand guests:
The carvèd angels, ever eager-eyed,
Stared, where upon their heads the cornice
    rests,
With hair blown back, and wings put cross-wise
  on their breasts.

V

At length burst in the argent revelry,
With plume, tiara, and all rich array,
Numerous as shadows haunting faerily
The brain, new-stuffed, in youth, with
    triumphs gay
Of old romance. These let us wish away,
And turn, sole-thoughted, to one Lady there,
Whose heart had brooded, all that wintry
    day,
On love, and winged St Agnes' saintly care,
As she had heard old dames full many times
  declare.

VI

They told her how, upon St Agnes' Eve,
Young virgins might have visions of delight,

· 191 ·

And soft adorings from their loves receive
Upon the honey'd middle of the night,
If ceremonies due they did aright;
As, supperless to bed they must retire,
And couch supine their beauties, lily white;
Nor look behind, nor sideways, but require
Of Heaven with upward eyes for all that they
    desire.

VII

Full of this whim was thoughtful Madeline:
The music, yearning like a God in pain,
She scarcely heard: her maiden eyes divine,
Fixed on the floor, saw many a sweeping train
Pass by – she heeded not at all: in vain
Came many a tip-toe, amorous cavalier,
And back retired – not cooled by high disdain,
But she saw not: her heart was otherwise.
She sighed for Agnes' dreams, the sweetest of
    the year.

VIII

She danced along with vague, regardless eyes,
Anxious her lips, her breathing quick and
    short:

The hallowed hour was near at hand: she sighs
Amid the timbrels, and the thronged resort
Of whisperers in anger, or in sport;
'Mid looks of love, defiance, hate, and scorn,
Hoodwinked with faery fancy – all amort,
Save to St Agnes and her lambs unshorn,
And all the bliss to be before to-morrow morn.

IX

So, purposing each moment to retire,
She lingered still. Meantime, across the
    moors,
Had come young Porphyro, with heart on fire
For Madeline. Beside the portal doors,
Buttressed from moonlight, stands he, and
    implores
All saints to give him sight of Madeline,
But for one moment in the tedious hours,
That he might gaze and worship all unseen;
Perchance speak, kneel, touch, kiss – in sooth
  such things have been.

X

He ventures in – let no buzzed whisper tell,
All eyes be muffled, or a hundred swords

Will storm his heart, Love's fev'rous citadel:
For him, those chambers held barbarian
      hordes,
Hyena foemen, and hot-blooded lords,
Whose very dogs would execrations howl
Against his lineage: not one breast affords
Him any mercy, in that mansion foul,
Save one old beldame, weak in body and in soul.

XI

Ah, happy chance! the agèd creature came,
Shuffling along with ivory-headed wand,
To where he stood, hid from the torch's
      flame,
Behind a broad hall-pillar, far beyond
The sound of merriment and chorus bland:
He startled her; but soon she knew his face,
And grasped his fingers in her palsied hand,
Saying, 'Mercy, Porphyro! hie thee from
      this place:
They are all here to-night, the whole blood-
      thirsty race!'

John Keats

MORE BEAUTIFUL THAN
MOON OR STAR

Stars and Moon

Beneath the stars and summer moon
A pair of wedded lovers walk,
Upon the stars and summer moon
They turn their happy eyes, and talk.

Coventry Patmore

She Was a Phantom of Delight

She was a Phantom of delight
When first she gleamed upon my sight;
A lovely Apparition, sent
To be a moment's ornament;
Her eyes as stars of Twilight fair;
Like Twilight's, too, her dusky hair;
But all things else about her drawn
From May-time and the cheerful Dawn;
A dancing Shape, an Image gay,
To haunt, to startle, and way-lay.
I saw her upon nearer view,
A Spirit, yet a Woman too!
Her household motions light and free,
And steps of virgin-liberty;
A countenance in which did meet
Sweet records, promises as sweet;
A Creature not too bright or good
For human nature's daily food;
For transient sorrows, simple wiles,
Praise, blame, love, kisses, tears, and smiles.
And now I see with eye serene
The very pulse of the machine;
A Being breathing thoughtful breath,

A Traveller between life and death;
The reason firm, the temperate will,
Endurance, foresight, strength, and skill;
A perfect Woman, nobly planned,
To warn, to comfort, and command;
And yet a Spirit still, and bright
With something of angelic light.

William Wordsworth

The cold earth slept below

The cold earth slept below;
  Above the cold sky shone;
    And all around,
    With a chilling sound,
From caves of ice and fields of snow
The breath of night like death did flow
    Beneath the sinking moon.

The wintry hedge was black;
  The green grass was not seen;
    The birds did rest
    On the bare thorn's breast,
Whose roots, beside the pathway track,
Had bound their folds o'er many a crack
    Which the frost had made between.

Thine eyes glow'd in the glare
  Of the moon's dying light;
    As a fen-fire's beam
    On a sluggish stream
Gleams dimly—so the moon shone there,
And it yellow'd the strings of thy tangled hair,
    That shook in the wind of night.

The moon made thy lips pale, beloved;
  The wind made thy bosom chill;
    The night did shed
    On thy dear head
Its frozen dew, and thou didst lie
Where the bitter breath of the naked sky
    Might visit thee at will.

Percy Bysshe Shelley

from The Princess

'Now sleeps the crimson petal, now the white;
Nor waves the cypress in the palace walk;
Nor winks the gold fin in the porphyry font:
The fire-fly wakens: waken thou with me.

Now droops the milkwhite peacock like a ghost,
And like a ghost she glimmers on to me.

Now lies the Earth all Danaë to the stars,
And all thy heart lies open unto me.

Now slides the silent meteor on, and leaves
A shining furrow, as thy thoughts in me.

Now folds the lily all her sweetness up,
And slips into the bosom of the lake:
So fold thyself, my dearest, thou, and slip
Into my bosom and be lost in me.'

Alfred, Lord Tennyson

She Walks in Beauty

I

She walks in beauty, like the night
   Of cloudless climes and starry skies;
And all that's best of dark and bright
   Meet in her aspect and her eyes:
Thus mellow'd to that tender light
   Which heaven to gaudy day denies.

II

One shade the more, one ray the less,
   Had half impair'd the nameless grace
Which waves in every raven tress,
   Or softly lightens o'er her face;
Where thoughts serenely sweet express,
   How pure, how dear their dwelling place.

III

And on that cheek, and o'er that brow,
   So soft, so calm, yet eloquent,
The smiles that win, the tints that glow,
   But tell of days in goodness spent,

A mind at peace with all below,
A heart whose love is innocent!

George, Lord Byron

Bright Star

Bright star! would I were steadfast as thou art –
   Not in lone splendour hung aloft the night
And watching, with eternal lids apart,
   Like nature's patient, sleepless Eremite,
The moving waters at their priestlike task
   Of pure ablution round earth's human shores,
Or gazing on the new soft-fallen mask
   Of snow upon the mountains and the moors –
No – yet still steadfast, still unchangeable,
   Pillowed upon my fair love's ripening breast,
To feel for ever its soft fall and swell,
   Awake for ever in a sweet unrest,
Still, still to hear her tender-taken breath,
And so live ever – or else swoon to death.

John Keats

The Possessed

The sun in crepe has muffled up his fire.
Moon of my life! Half shade yourself like him.
Slumber or smoke. Be silent and be dim,
And in the gulf of boredom plunge entire;

I love you thus! However, if you like,
Like some bright star from its eclipse emerging,
To flaunt with Folly where the crowds are surging—
Flash, lovely dagger, from your sheath and
   strike!

Light up your eyes from chandeliers of glass!
Light up the lustful looks of louts that pass!
Morbid or petulant, I thrill before you.

Be what you will, black night or crimson dawn;
No fibre of my body tautly-drawn,
But cries: "Beloved demon, I adore you!"

Charles Baudelaire

An Invite, to Eternity

Wilt thou go with me, sweet maid,
Say, maiden, wilt thou go with me
Through the valley-depths of shade,
Of night and dark obscurity;
Where the path has lost its way,
Where the sun forgets the day,
Where there's nor life nor light to see,
Sweet maiden, wilt thou go with me!

Where stones will turn to flooding streams,
Where plains will rise like ocean waves,
Where life will fade like visioned dreams
And mountains darken into caves,
Say, maiden, wilt thou go with me
Through this sad non-identity,
Where parents live and are forgot,
And sisters live and know us not!

Say, maiden; wilt thou go with me
In this strange death of life to be,
To live in death and be the same,
Without this life or home or name,
At once to be and not to be –

That was and is not – yet to see
Things pass like shadows, and the sky
Above, below, around us lie?

The land of shadows wilt thou trace
And look nor know each other's face.
The present mixed with reasons gone,
And past and present all as one.
Say maiden, can thy life be led
To join the living to the dead?
Then trace thy footsteps on with me,
We're wed to one eternity.

John Clare

A Song by the Shore

"Lose and love" is love's first art;
So it was with thee and me,
For I first beheld thy heart
On the night I last saw thee.
Pine-woods and mysteries!
Sea-sands and sorrows!
Hearts fluttered by a breeze
That bodes dark morrows, morrows,—
Bodes dark morrows!

Moonlight in sweet overflow
Poured upon the earth and sea!
Lovelight with intenser glow
In the deeps of thee and me!
Clasped hands and silences!
Hearts faint and throbbing!
The weak wind sighing in the trees!
The strong surf sobbing, sobbing,—
The strong surf sobbing!

Richard Hovey

If death is kind

Perhaps if Death is kind, and there can be
  returning,
We will come back to earth some fragrant night,
And take these lanes to find the sea, and
  bending
Breathe the same honeysuckle, low and white.

We will come down at night to these
  resounding beaches
And the long gentle thunder of the sea,
Here for a single hour in the wide starlight
We shall be happy, for the dead are free.

Sara Teasdale

Epilogue

And so I said to him:
Go—
into the ether,
into the boundless waters,
into the tempest,
into the celestial expanse,
wherever you may be.
Make of it your spirit-tomb,
roam free.

But wait for me.
For I will find you there someday,
my shadow,
my phantom,
my ghost,
in everlasting love.

Charlie Castelletti

Index of Poets and Authors

Permissions Acknowledgements